Pea, Bee, & Jay

STUCK TOGETHER

Brian "Smitty" Smith

HARPER alley

An Imprint of HarperCollinsPublishers

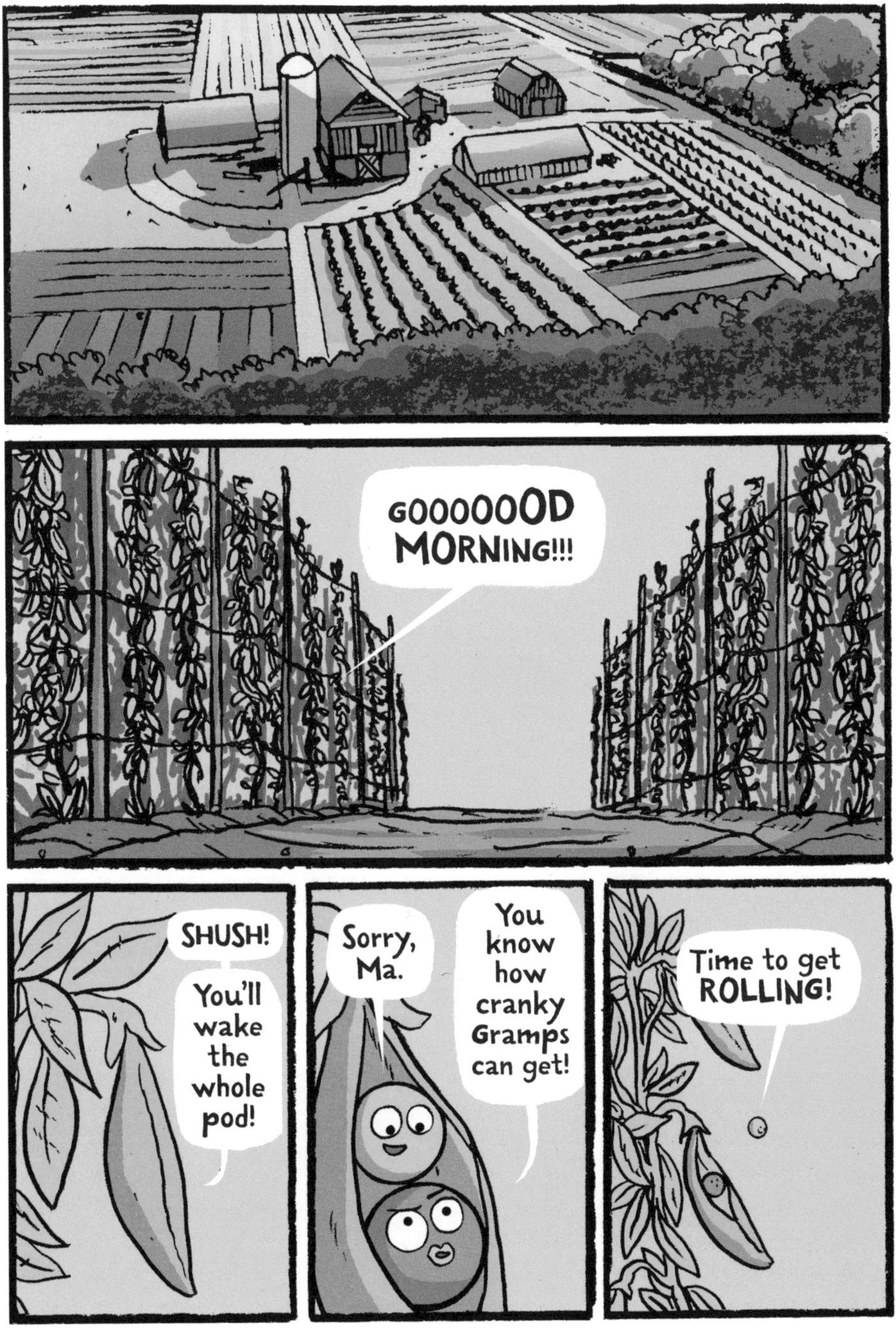
GOOOOOOD MORNING!!!
SHUSH!
You'll wake the whole pod!
Sorry, Ma.
You know how cranky Gramps can get!
Time to get ROLLING!

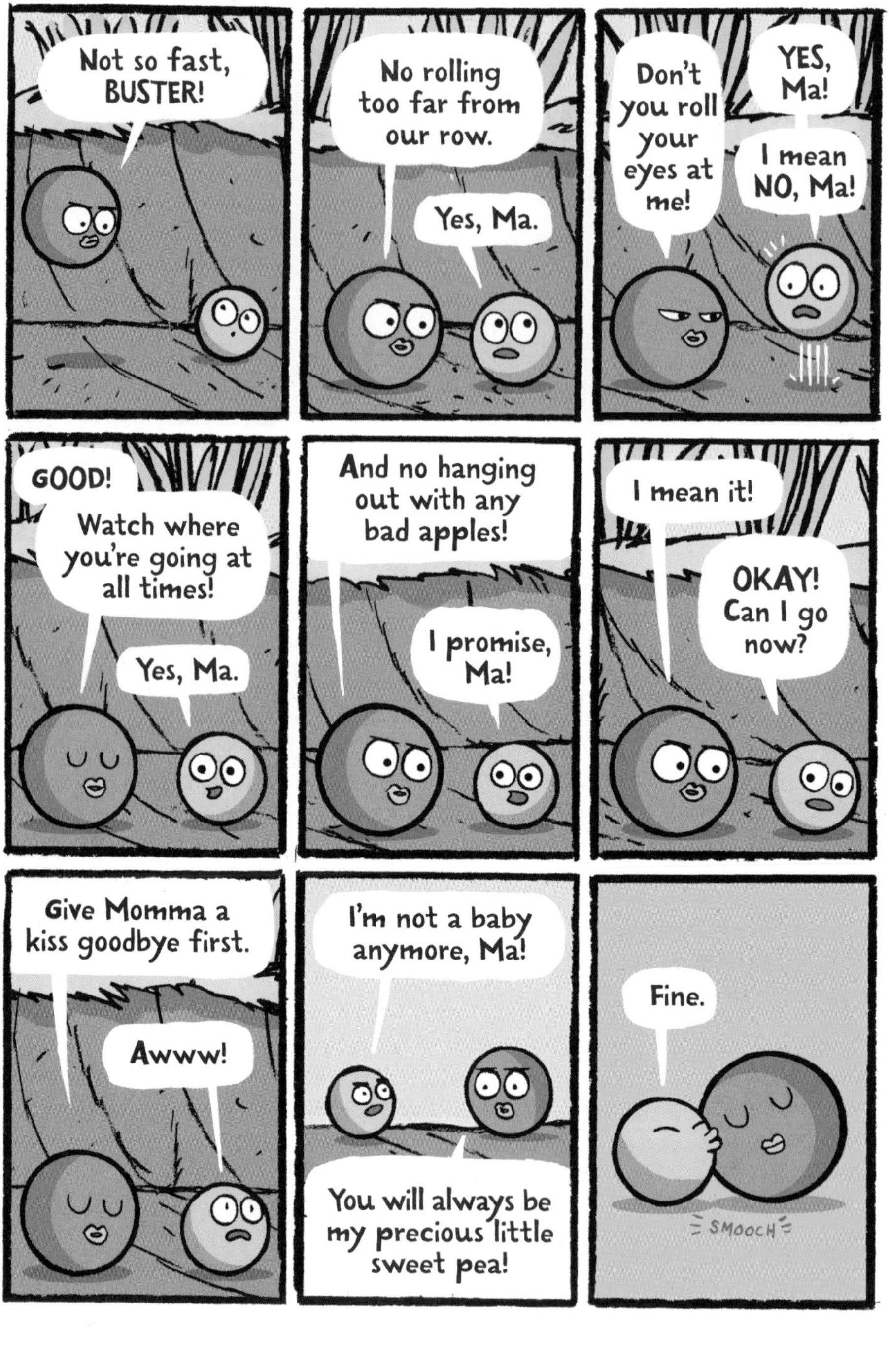
Not so fast, BUSTER!
No rolling too far from our row.
Yes, Ma.
Don't you roll your eyes at me!
YES, Ma!
I mean NO, Ma!
GOOD!
Watch where you're going at all times!
Yes, Ma.
And no hanging out with any bad apples!
I promise, Ma!
I mean it!
OKAY! Can I go now?
Give Momma a kiss goodbye first.
Awww!
I'm not a baby anymore, Ma!
You will always be my precious little sweet pea!
Fine.
SMOOCH

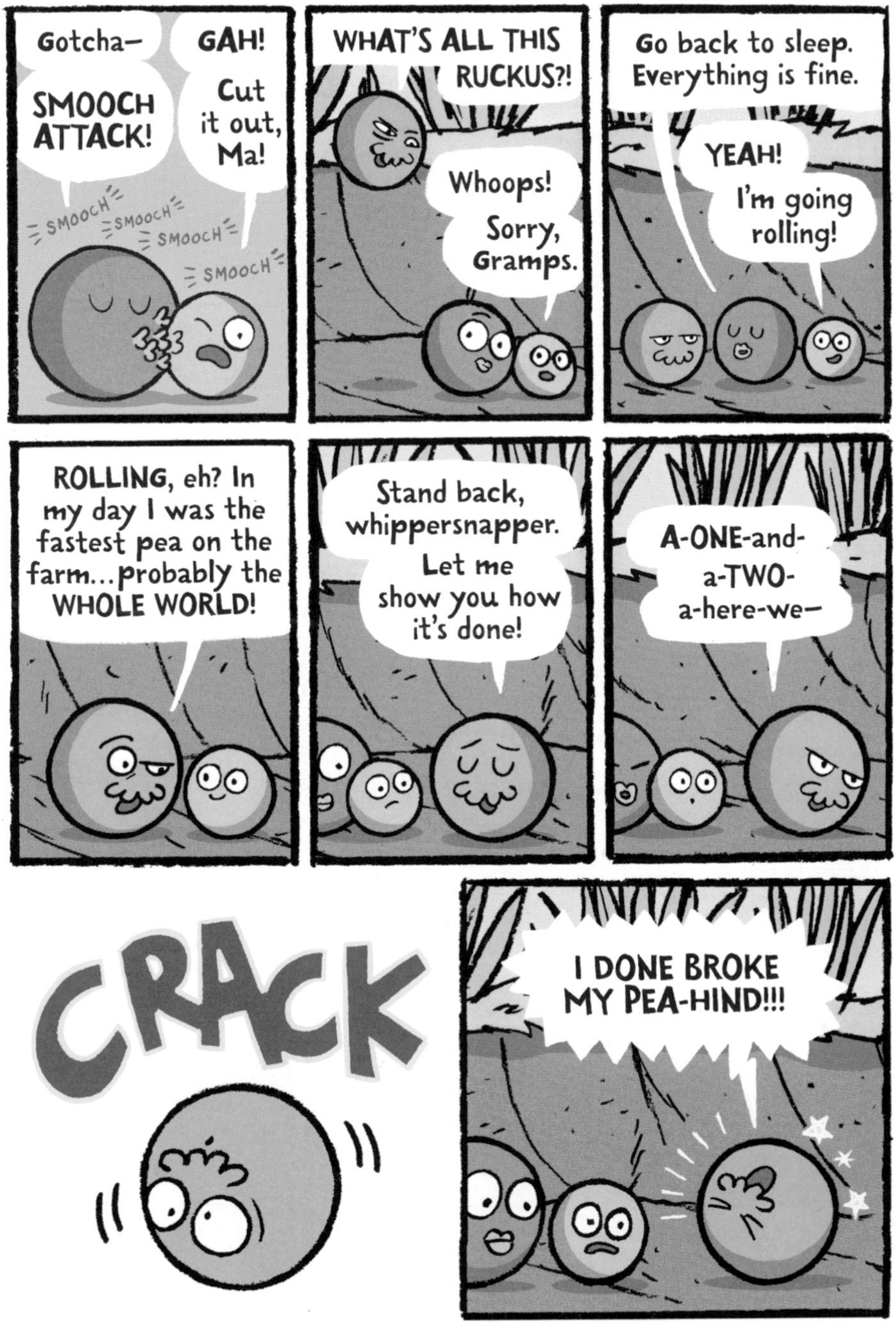
Gotcha—
SMOOCH ATTACK!
GAH!
Cut it out, Ma!
SMOOCH SMOOCH SMOOCH
SMOOCH
WHAT'S ALL THIS RUCKUS?!
Whoops!
Sorry, Gramps.
Go back to sleep. Everything is fine.
YEAH!
I'm going rolling!
ROLLING, eh? In my day I was the fastest pea on the farm...probably the WHOLE WORLD!
Stand back, whippersnapper.
Let me show you how it's done!
A-ONE-and-a-TWO-a-here-we—
CRACK
I DONE BROKE MY PEA-HIND!!!

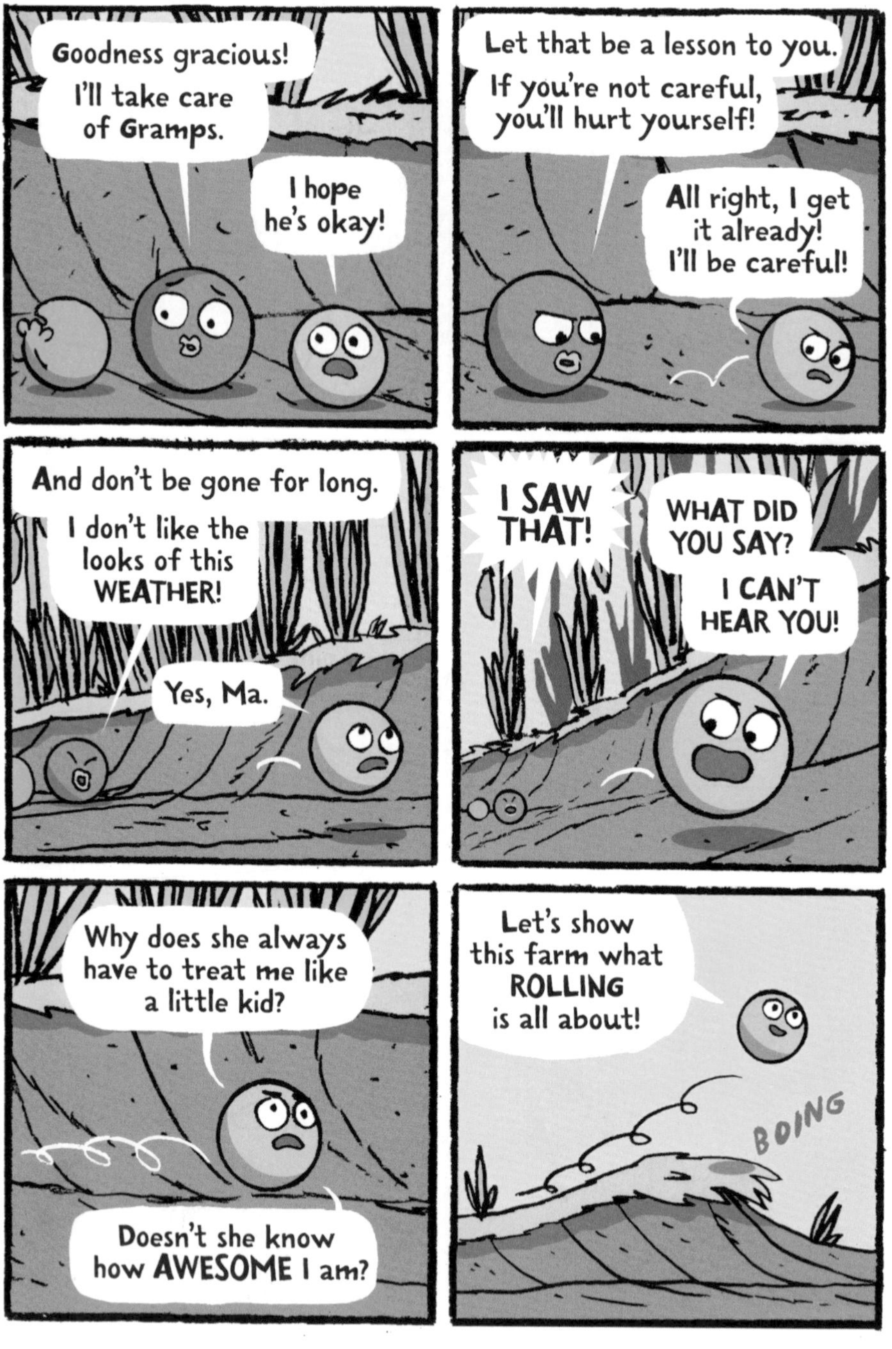

Goodness gracious!
I'll take care of Gramps.
I hope he's okay!
Let that be a lesson to you.
If you're not careful, you'll hurt yourself!
All right, I get it already! I'll be careful!
And don't be gone for long.
I don't like the looks of this WEATHER!
Yes, Ma.
I SAW THAT!
WHAT DID YOU SAY?
I CAN'T HEAR YOU!
Why does she always have to treat me like a little kid?
Doesn't she know how AWESOME I am?
Let's show this farm what ROLLING is all about!
BOING

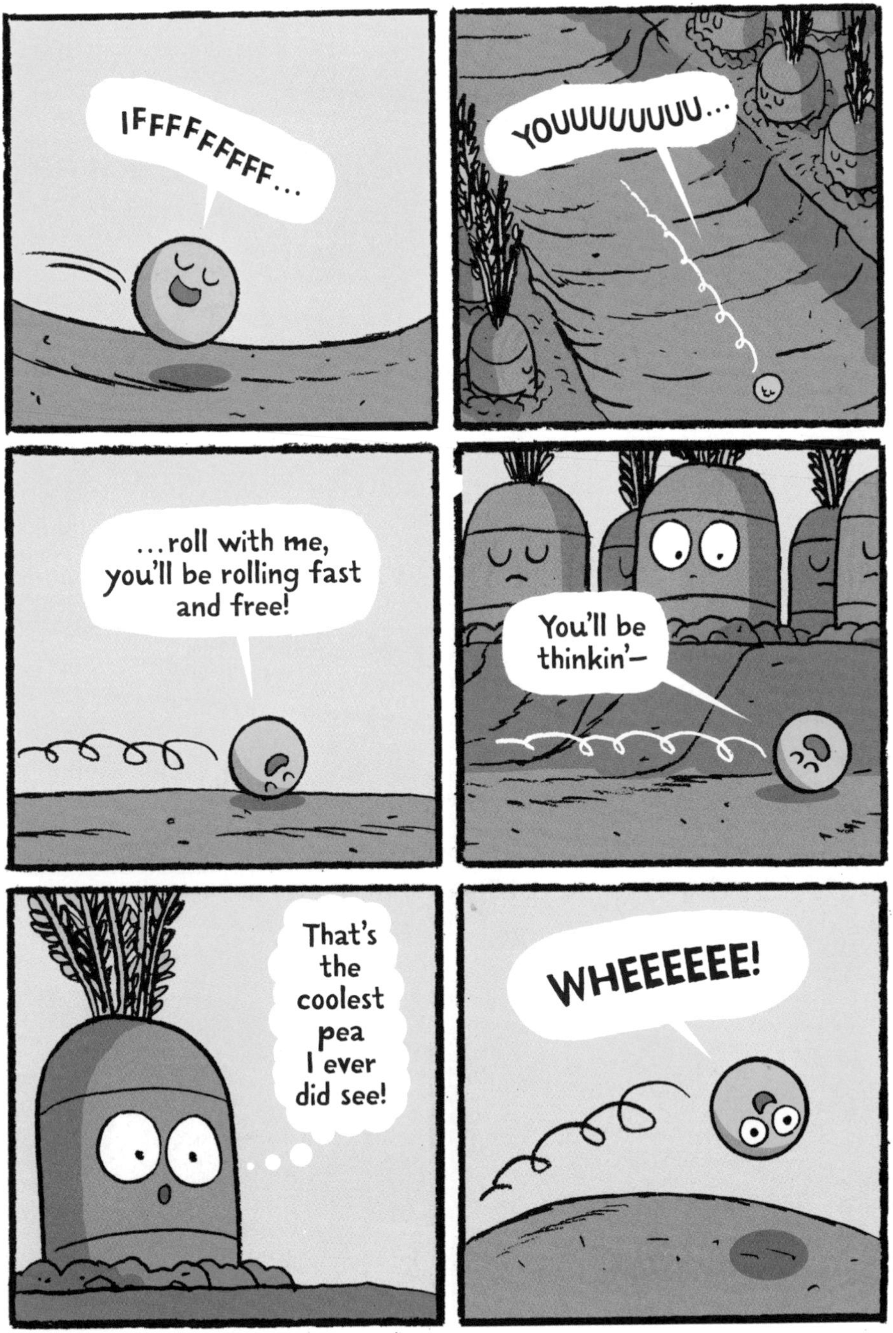
IFFFFFFFFF...
YOUUUUUUUU...
...roll with me, you'll be rolling fast and free!
You'll be thinkin'–
That's the coolest pea I ever did see!
WHEEEEEE!

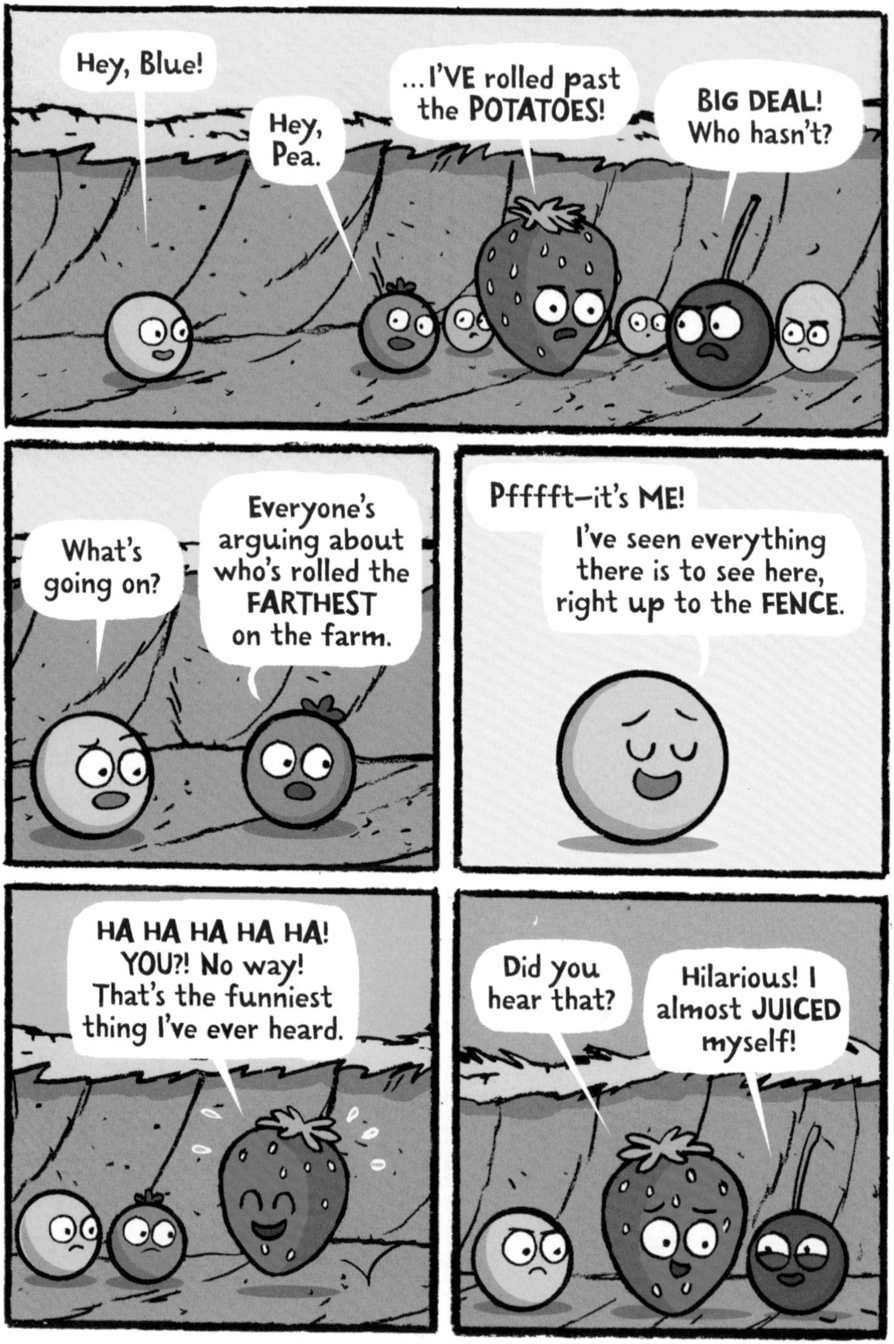
Hey, Blue!
Hey, Pea.
...I'VE rolled past the POTATOES!
BIG DEAL! Who hasn't?
What's going on?
Everyone's arguing about who's rolled the FARTHEST on the farm.
Pffft–it's ME!
I've seen everything there is to see here, right up to the FENCE.
HA HA HA HA HA! YOU?! No way! That's the funniest thing I've ever heard.
Did you hear that?
Hilarious! I almost JUICED myself!

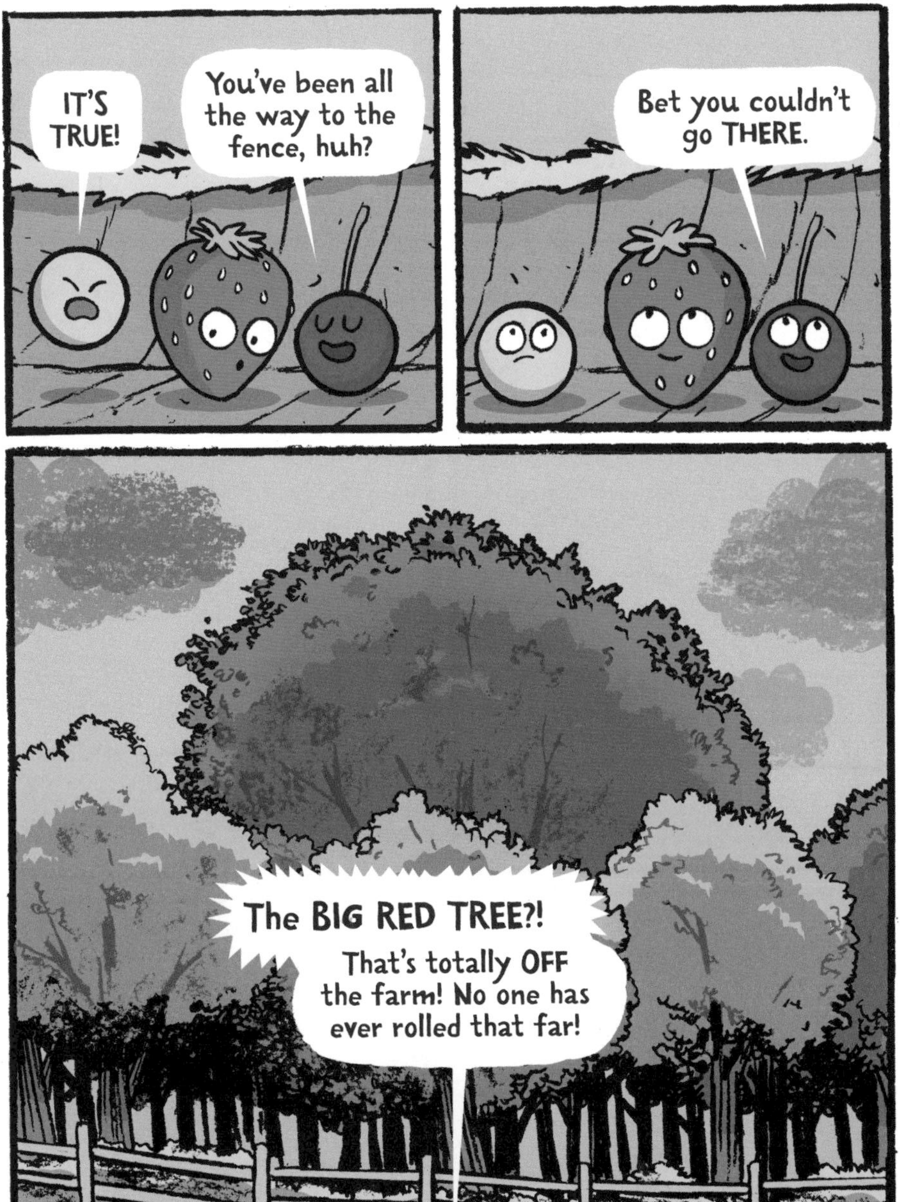
IT'S TRUE!
You've been all the way to the fence, huh?
Bet you couldn't go THERE.
The BIG RED TREE?!
That's totally OFF the farm! No one has ever rolled that far!

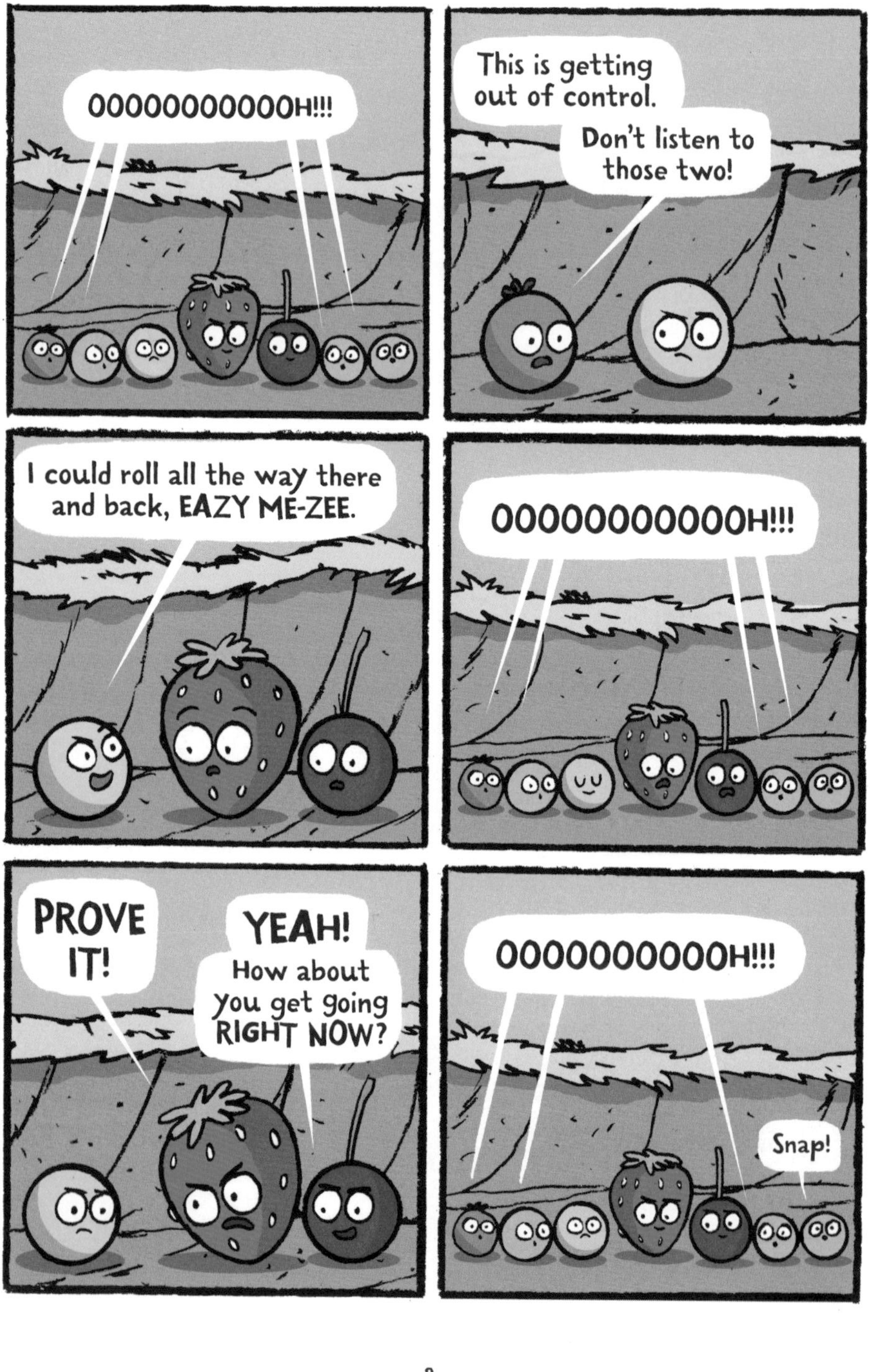
OOOOOOOOOOOH!!!
This is getting out of control.
Don't listen to those two!
I could roll all the way there and back, EAZY ME-ZEE.
OOOOOOOOOOOH!!!
PROVE IT!
YEAH! How about you get going RIGHT NOW?
OOOOOOOOOOH!!!
Snap!

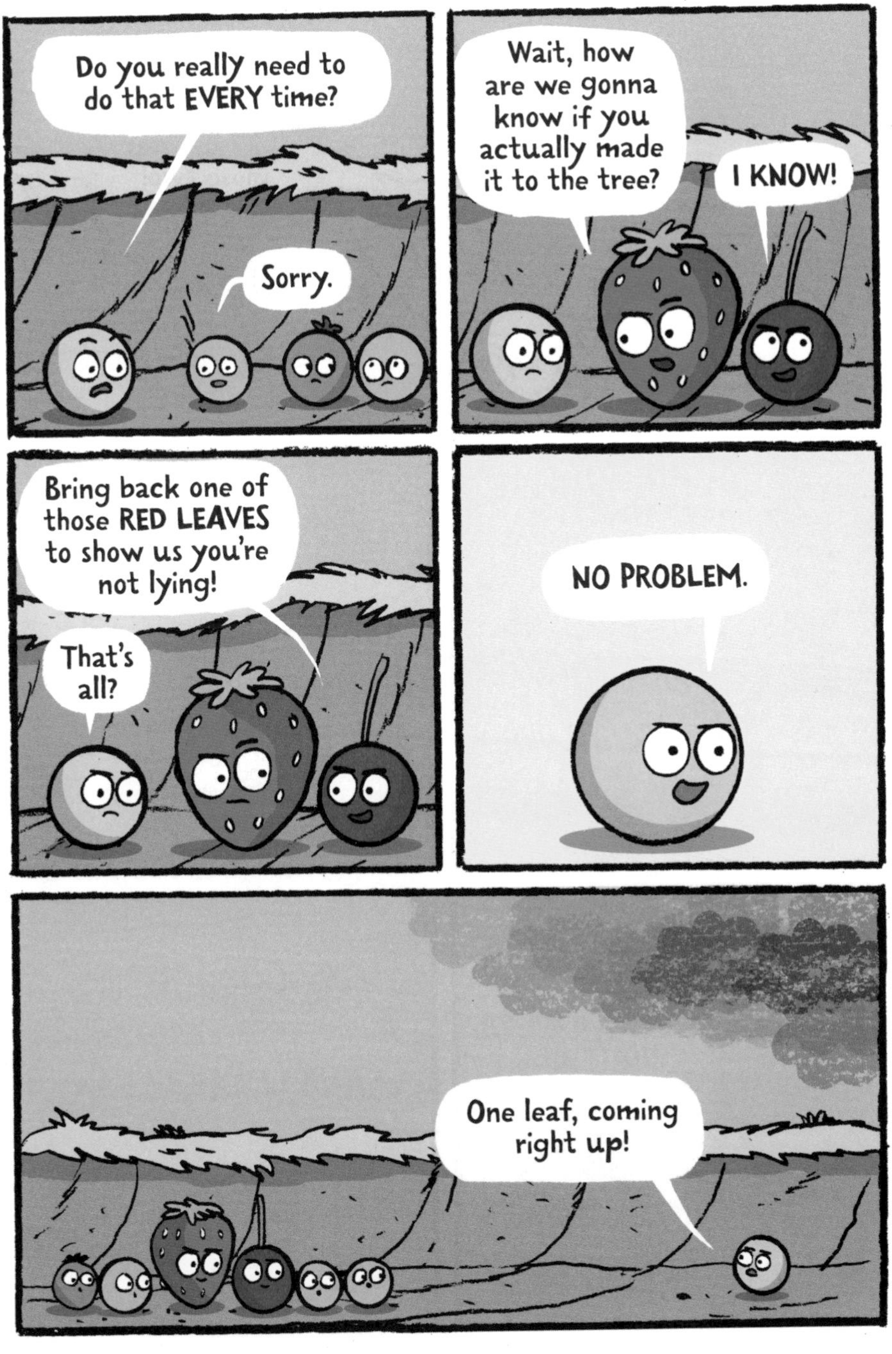
Do you really need to do that EVERY time?
Sorry.
Wait, how are we gonna know if you actually made it to the tree?
I KNOW!
Bring back one of those RED LEAVES to show us you're not lying!
That's all?
NO PROBLEM.
One leaf, coming right up!

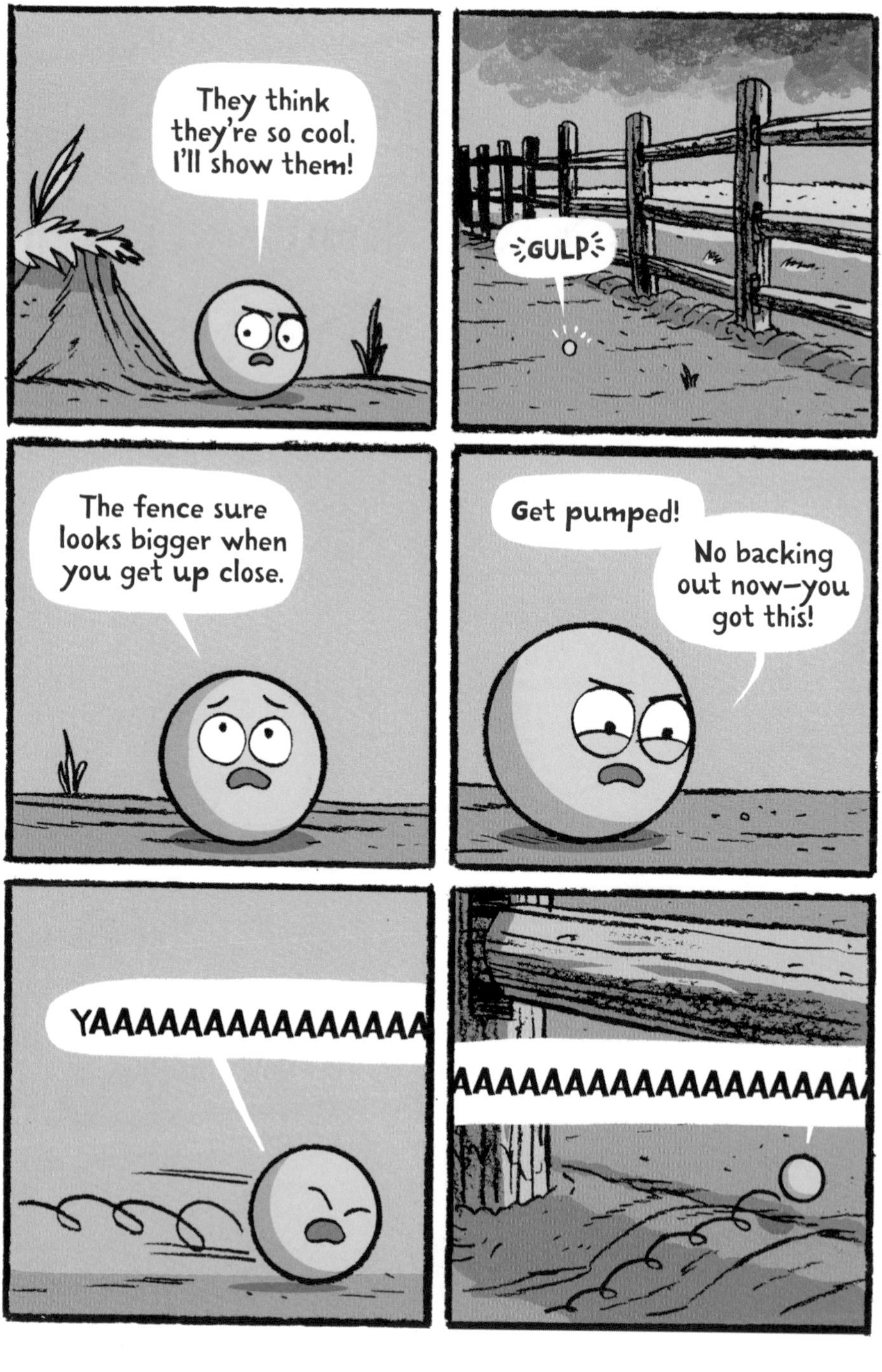
They think they're so cool. I'll show them!
GULP
The fence sure looks bigger when you get up close.
Get pumped!
No backing out now—you got this!
YAAAAAAAAAAAAAAAA
AAAAAAAAAAAAAAAAAAAAA

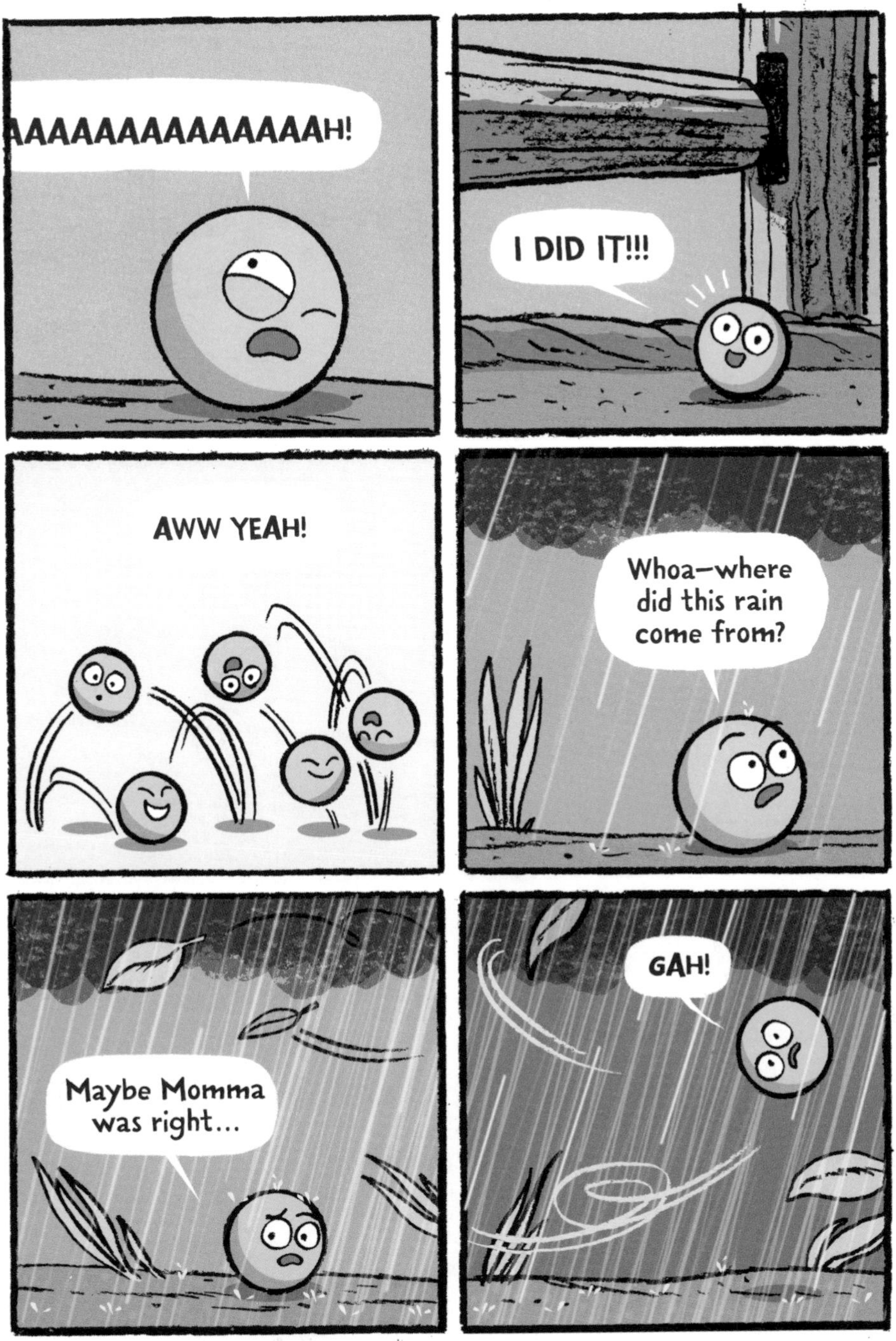
AAAAAAAAAAAAAAAH!
I DID IT!!!
AWW YEAH!
Whoa—where did this rain come from?
Maybe Momma was right...
GAH!

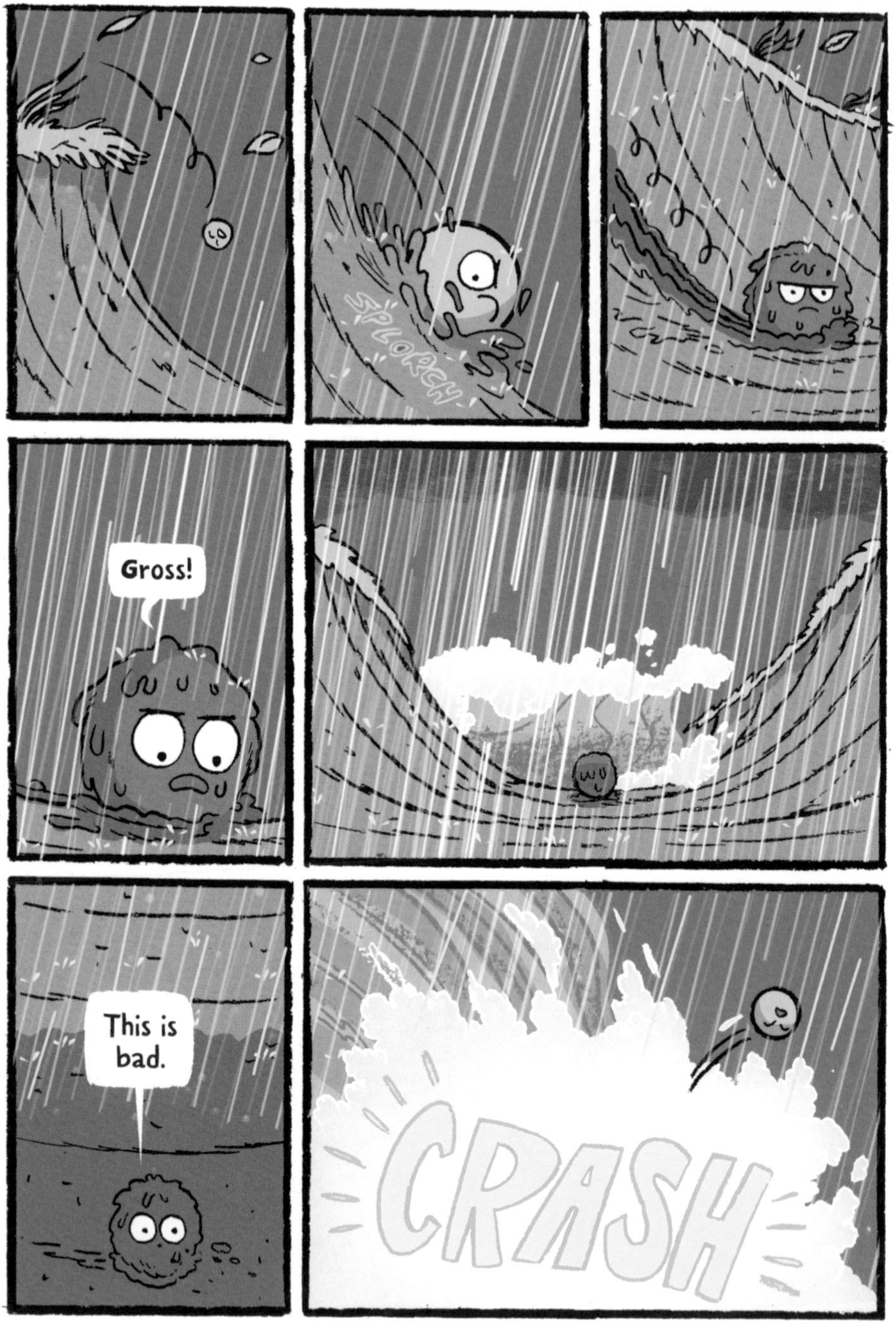
SPLORCH
Gross!
This is bad.
CRASH

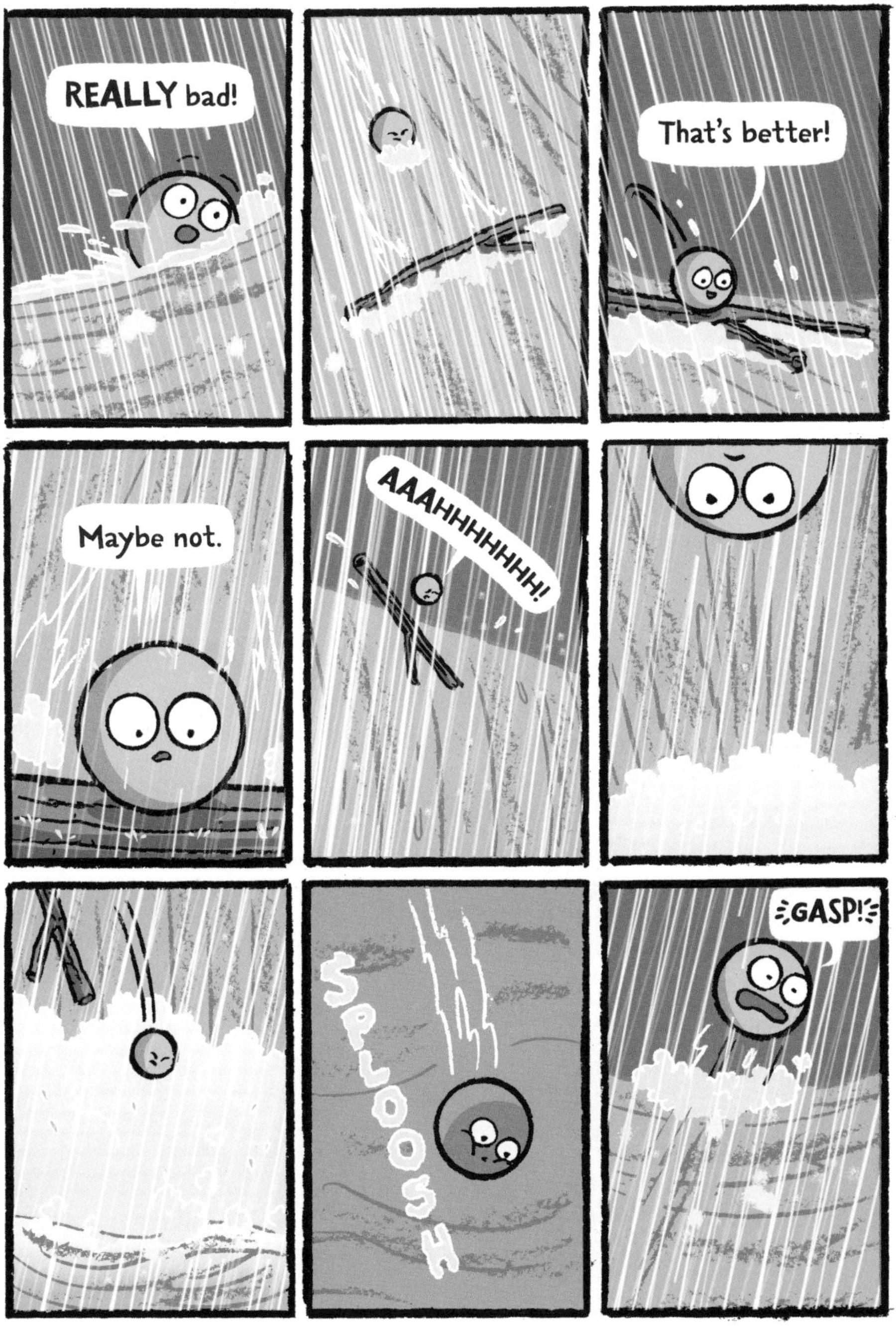
REALLY bad!
That's better!
Maybe not.
AAAHHHHHHH!
SPLOOSH
GASP!

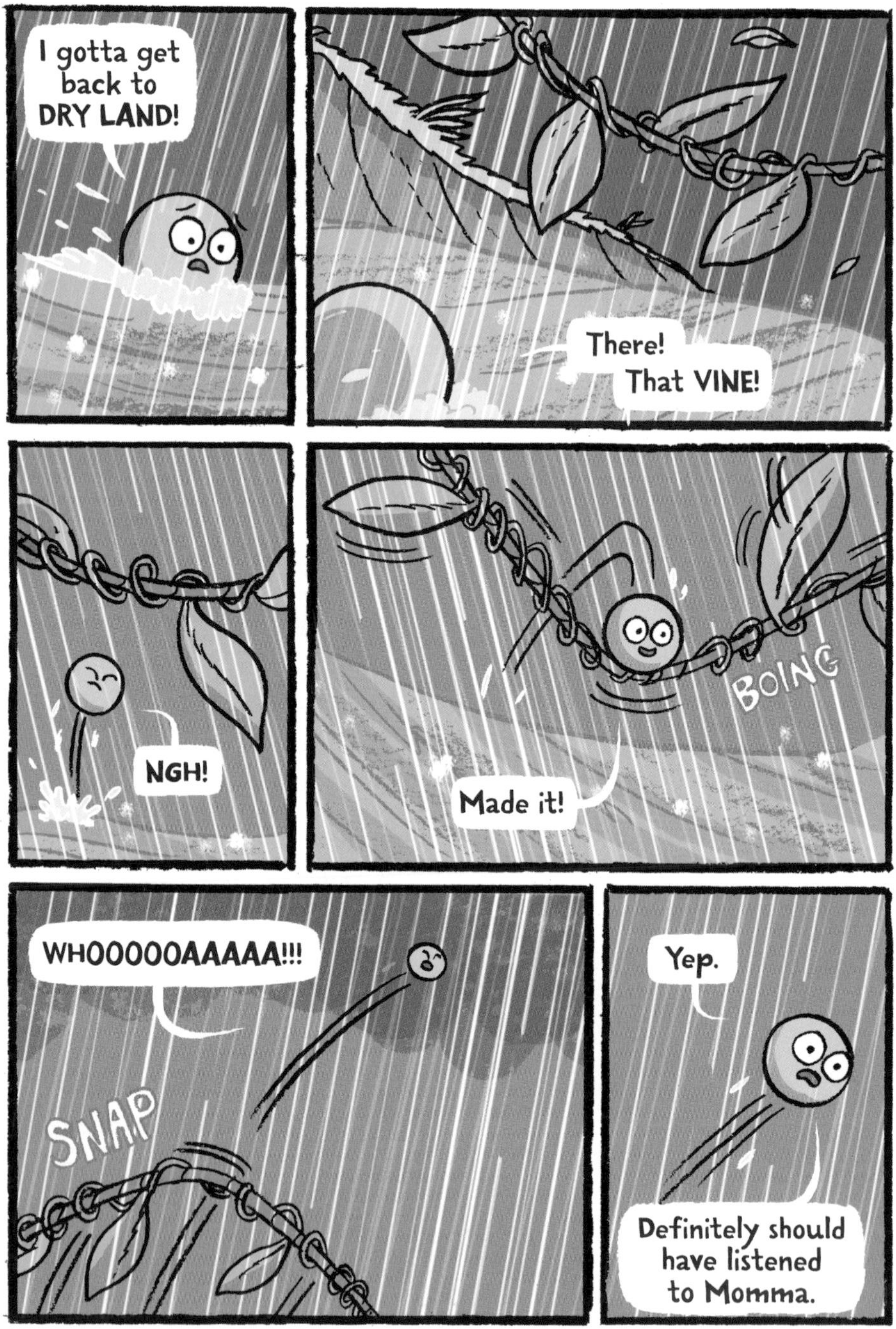
I gotta get back to DRY LAND!
There! That VINE!
NGH!
Made it!
BOING
WHOOOOOAAAAA!!!
SNAP
Yep.
Definitely should have listened to Momma.

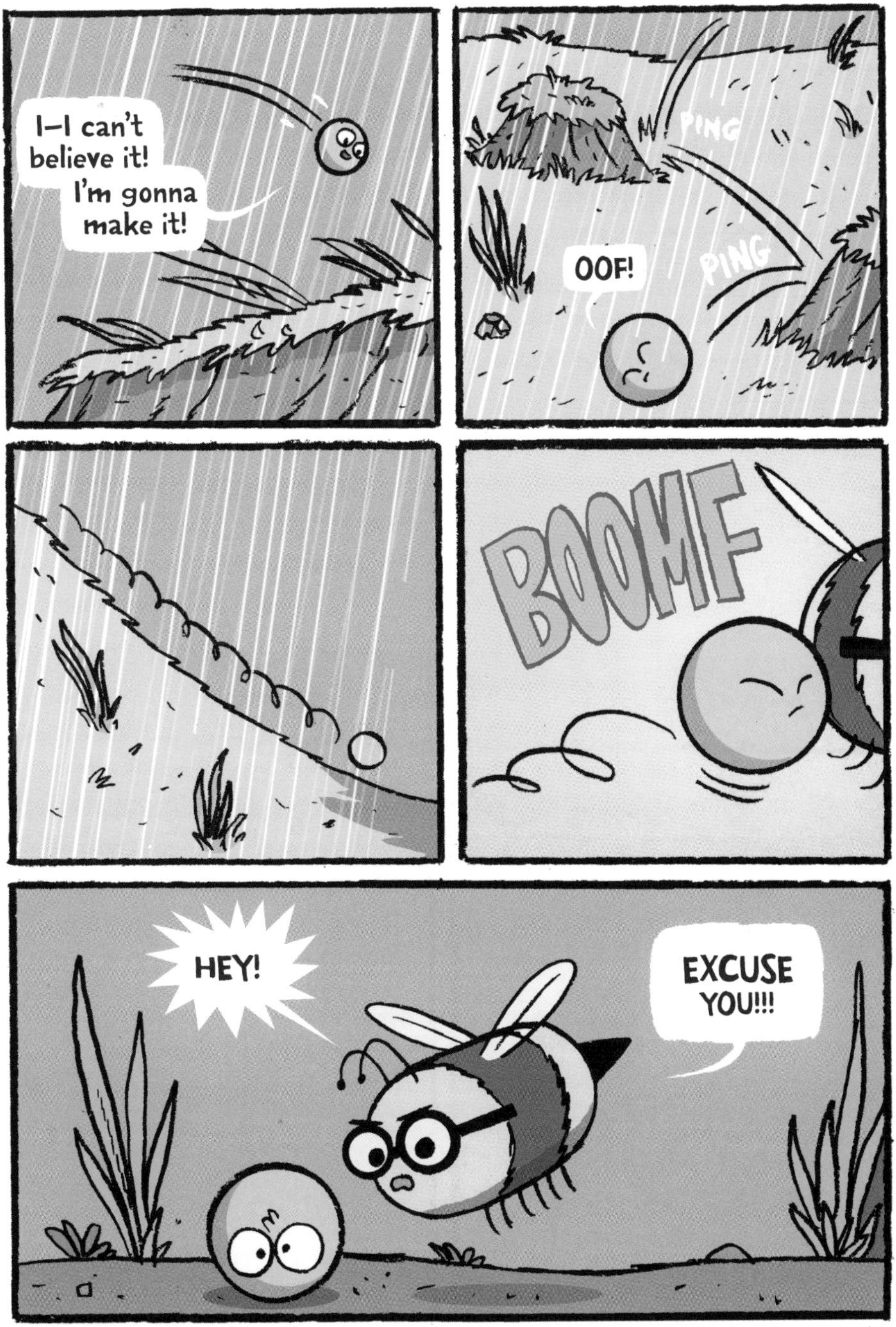
I–I can't believe it!
I'm gonna make it!
PING
PING
OOF!
BOOMF
HEY!
EXCUSE YOU!!!

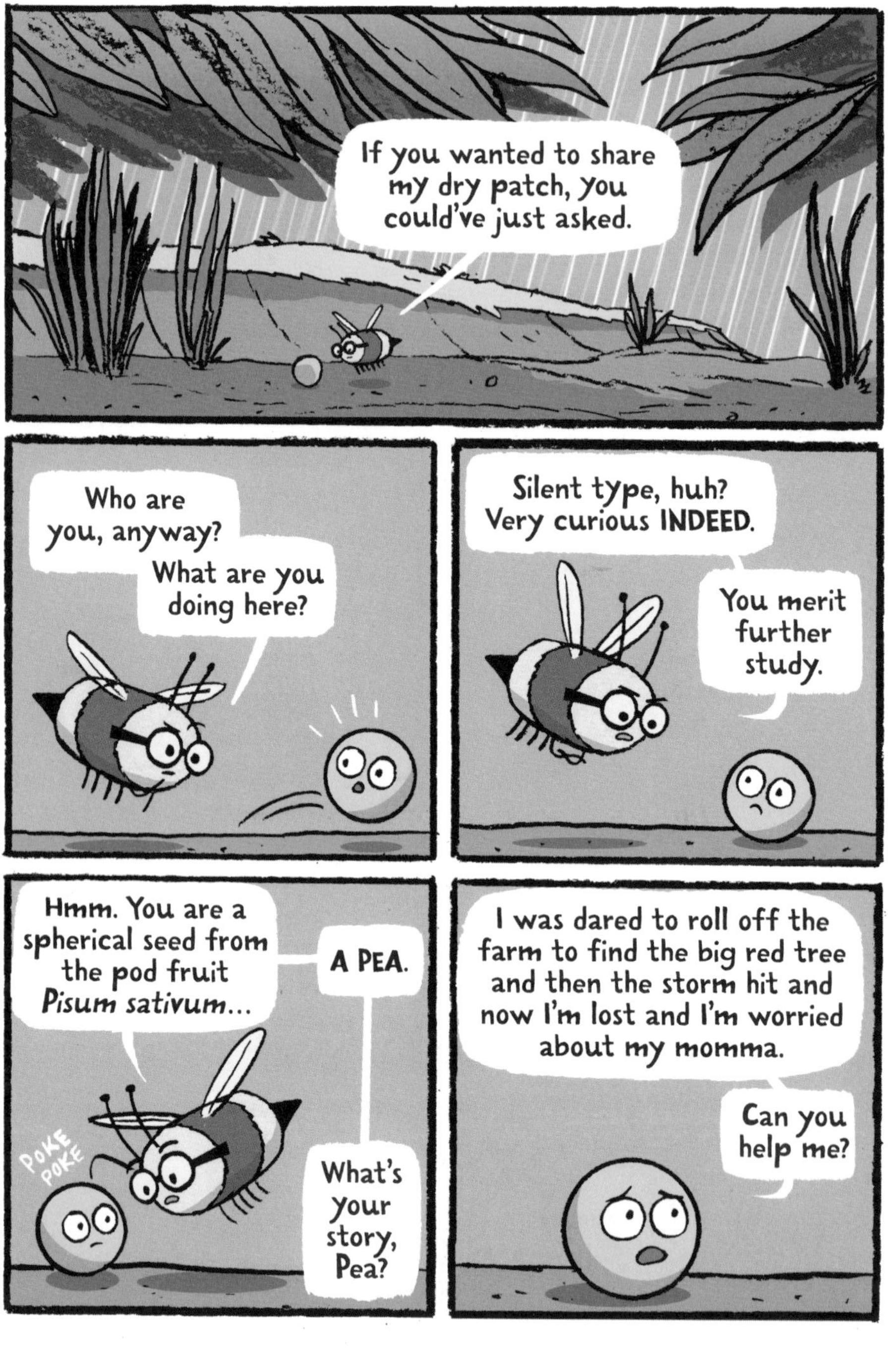

If you wanted to share my dry patch, you could've just asked.
Who are you, anyway?
What are you doing here?
Silent type, huh? Very curious INDEED.
You merit further study.
Hmm. You are a spherical seed from the pod fruit *Pisum sativum*...
A PEA.
What's your story, Pea?
POKE POKE
I was dared to roll off the farm to find the big red tree and then the storm hit and now I'm lost and I'm worried about my momma.
Can you help me?

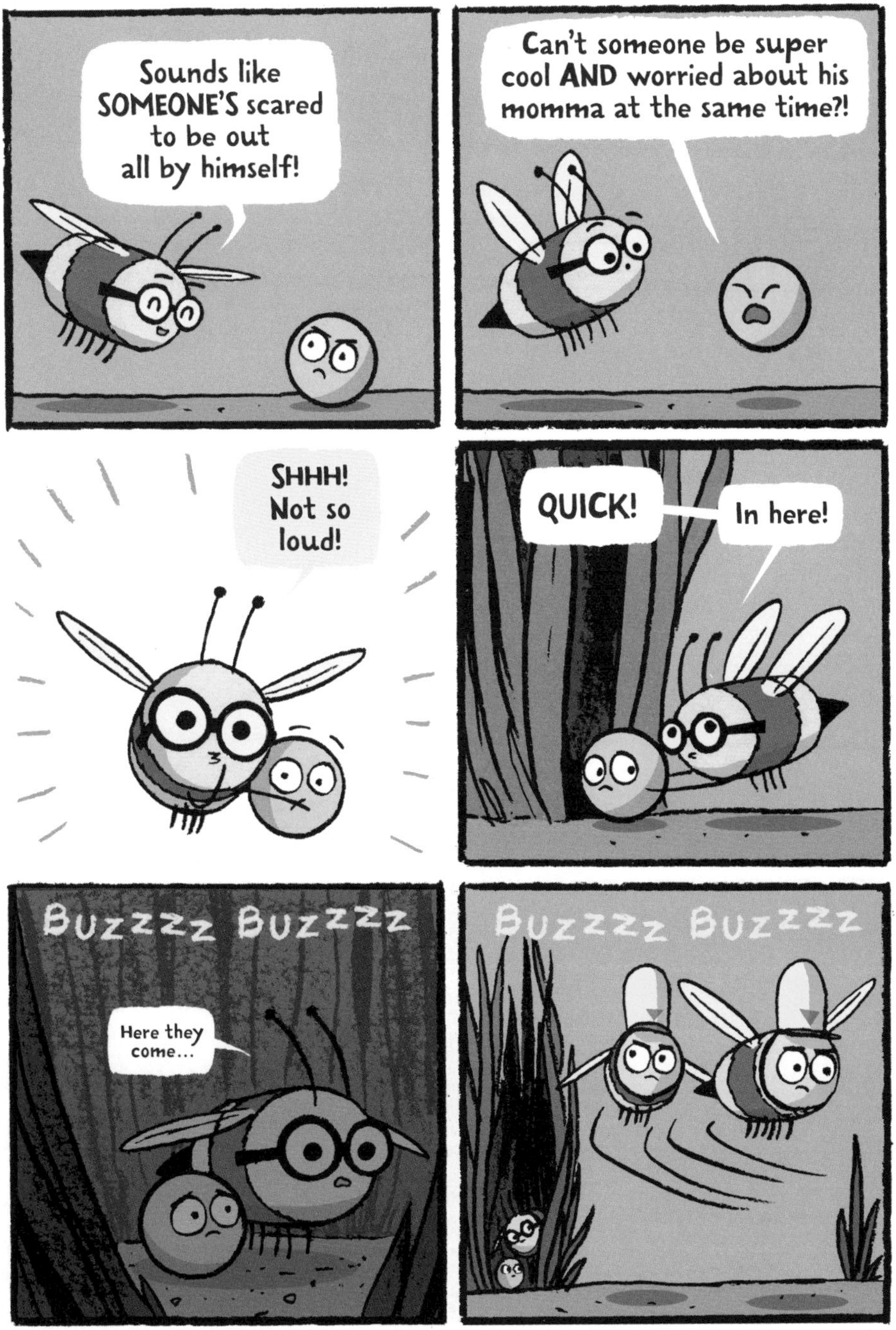
Sounds like SOMEONE'S scared to be out all by himself!
Can't someone be super cool AND worried about his momma at the same time?!
SHHH! Not so loud!
QUICK!
In here!
BUZZZZ BUZZZZ
Here they come...
BUZZZZ BUZZZZ

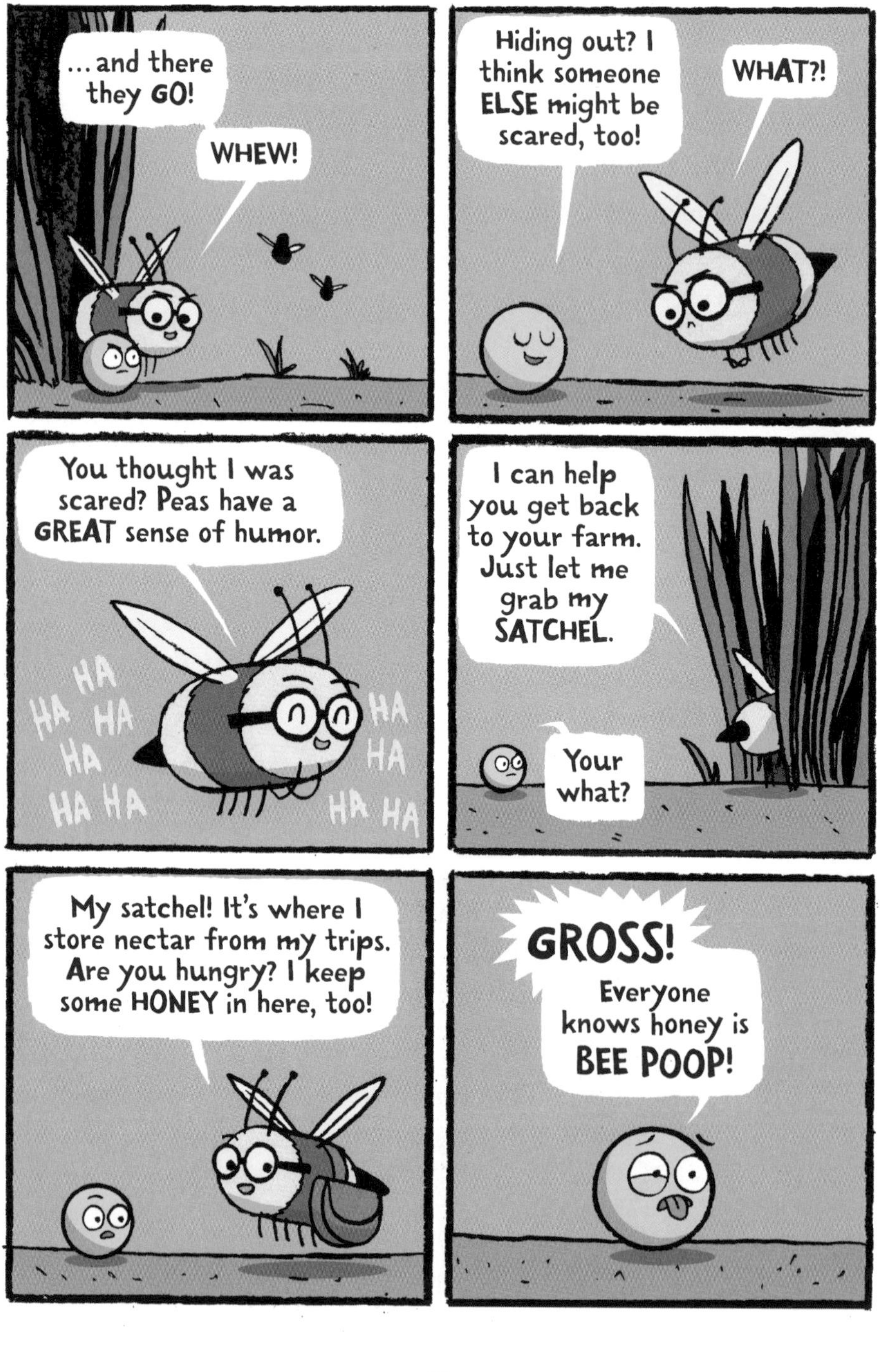
...and there they GO!
WHEW!
Hiding out? I think someone ELSE might be scared, too!
WHAT?!
You thought I was scared? Peas have a GREAT sense of humor.
HA HA HA HA HA HA HA HA HA HA HA HA
I can help you get back to your farm. Just let me grab my SATCHEL.
Your what?
My satchel! It's where I store nectar from my trips. Are you hungry? I keep some HONEY in here, too!
GROSS!
Everyone knows honey is BEE POOP!

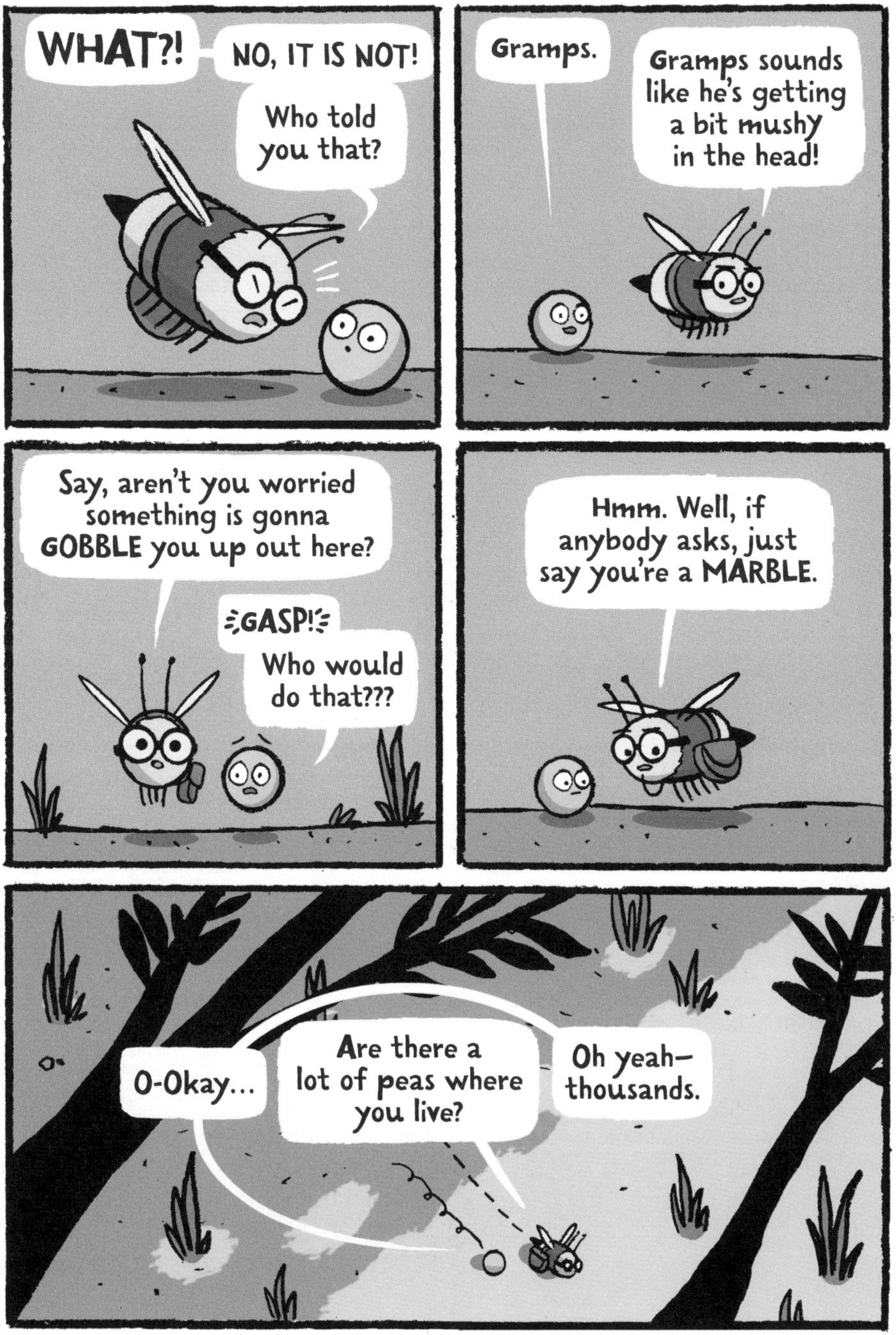
WHAT?!
NO, IT IS NOT!
Who told you that?
Gramps.
Gramps sounds like he's getting a bit mushy in the head!
Say, aren't you worried something is gonna GOBBLE you up out here?
GASP!
Who would do that???
Hmm. Well, if anybody asks, just say you're a MARBLE.
O-Okay...
Are there a lot of peas where you live?
Oh yeah— thousands.

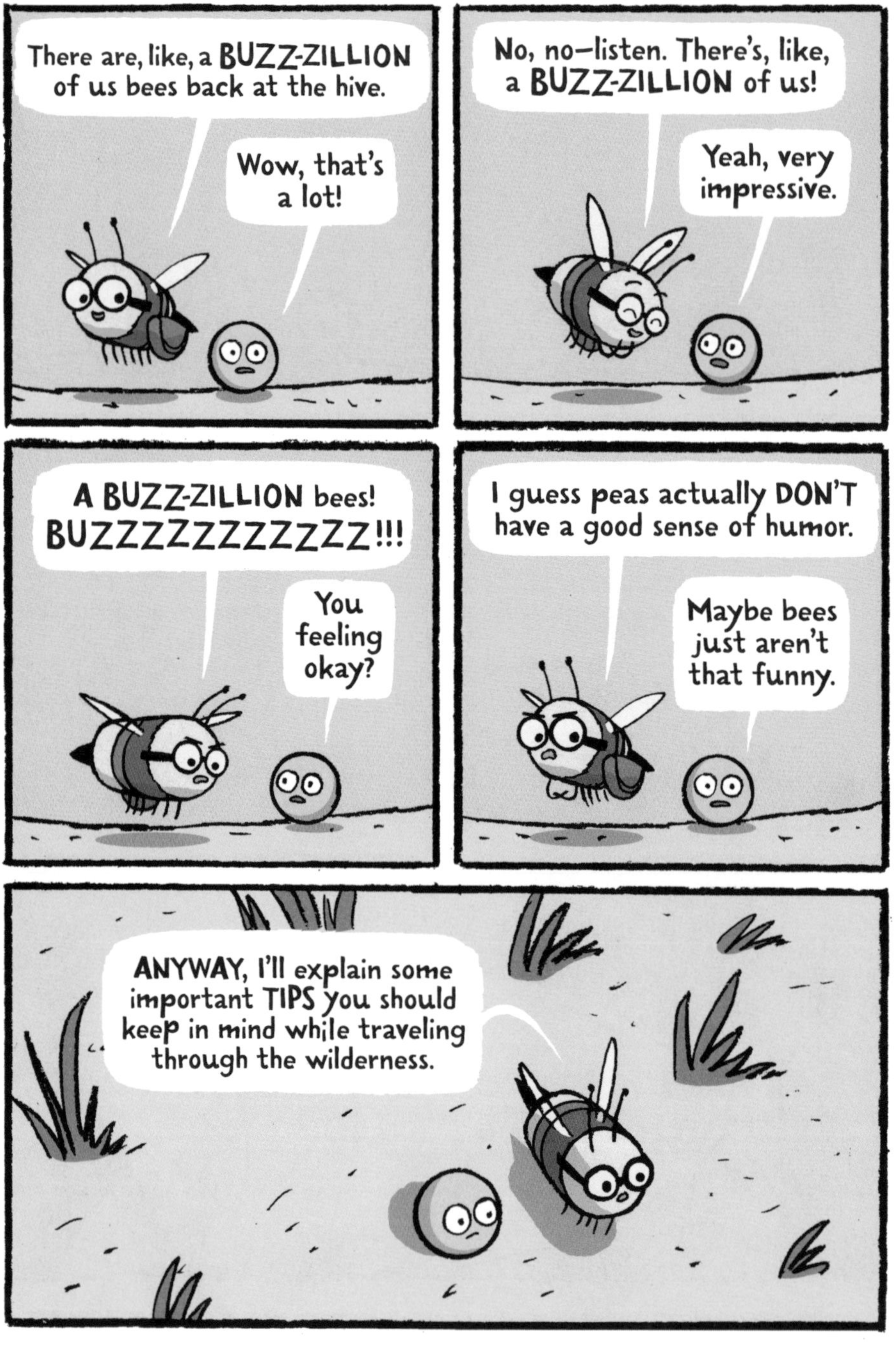
There are, like, a BUZZ-ZILLION of us bees back at the hive.
Wow, that's a lot!
No, no—listen. There's, like, a BUZZ-ZILLION of us!
Yeah, very impressive.
A BUZZ-ZILLION bees! BUZZZZZZZZZZZ!!!
You feeling okay?
I guess peas actually DON'T have a good sense of humor.
Maybe bees just aren't that funny.
ANYWAY, I'll explain some important TIPS you should keep in mind while traveling through the wilderness.

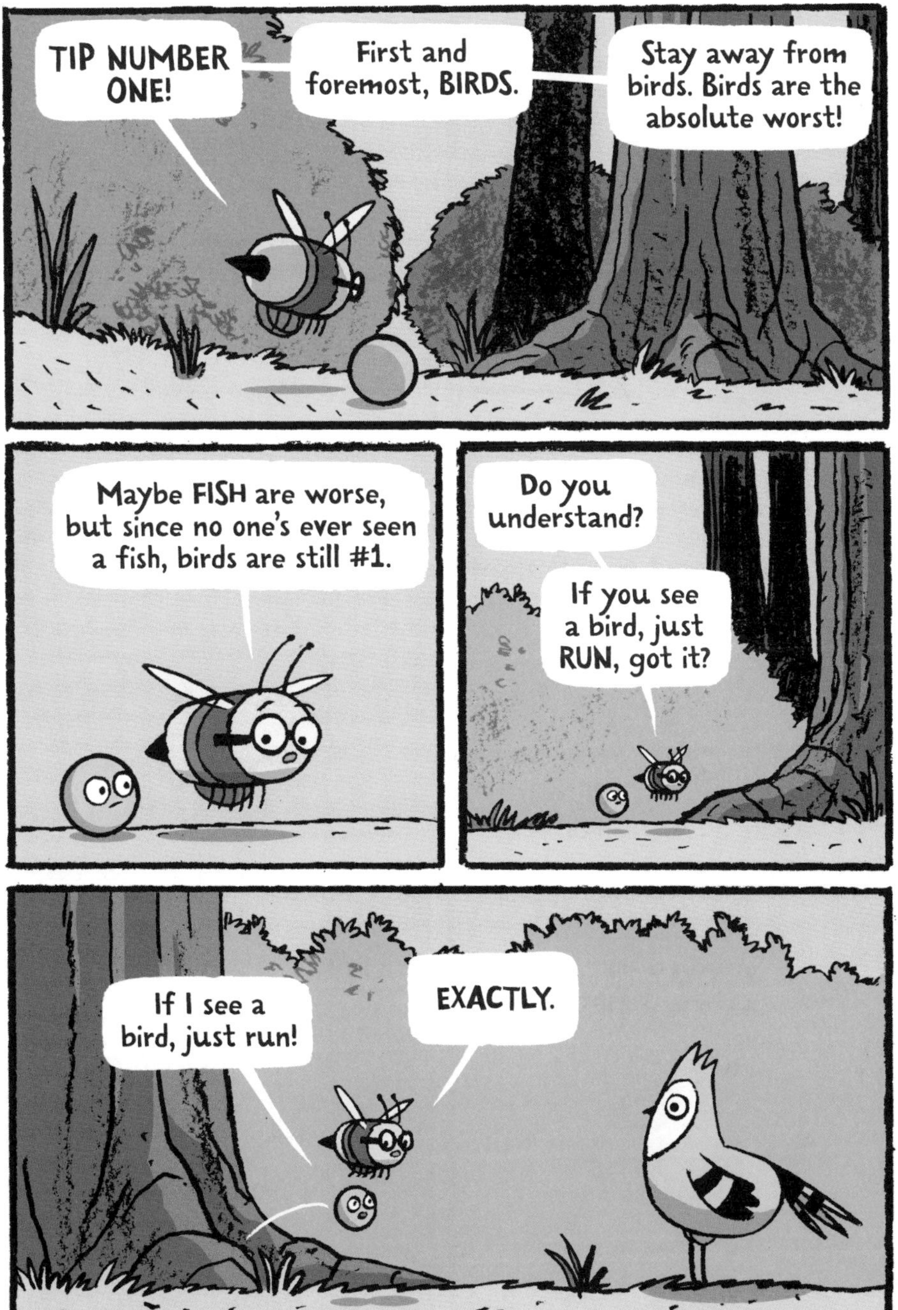
TIP NUMBER ONE!
First and foremost, BIRDS.
Stay away from birds. Birds are the absolute worst!
Maybe FISH are worse, but since no one's ever seen a fish, birds are still #1.
Do you understand?
If you see a bird, just RUN, got it?
If I see a bird, just run!
EXACTLY.

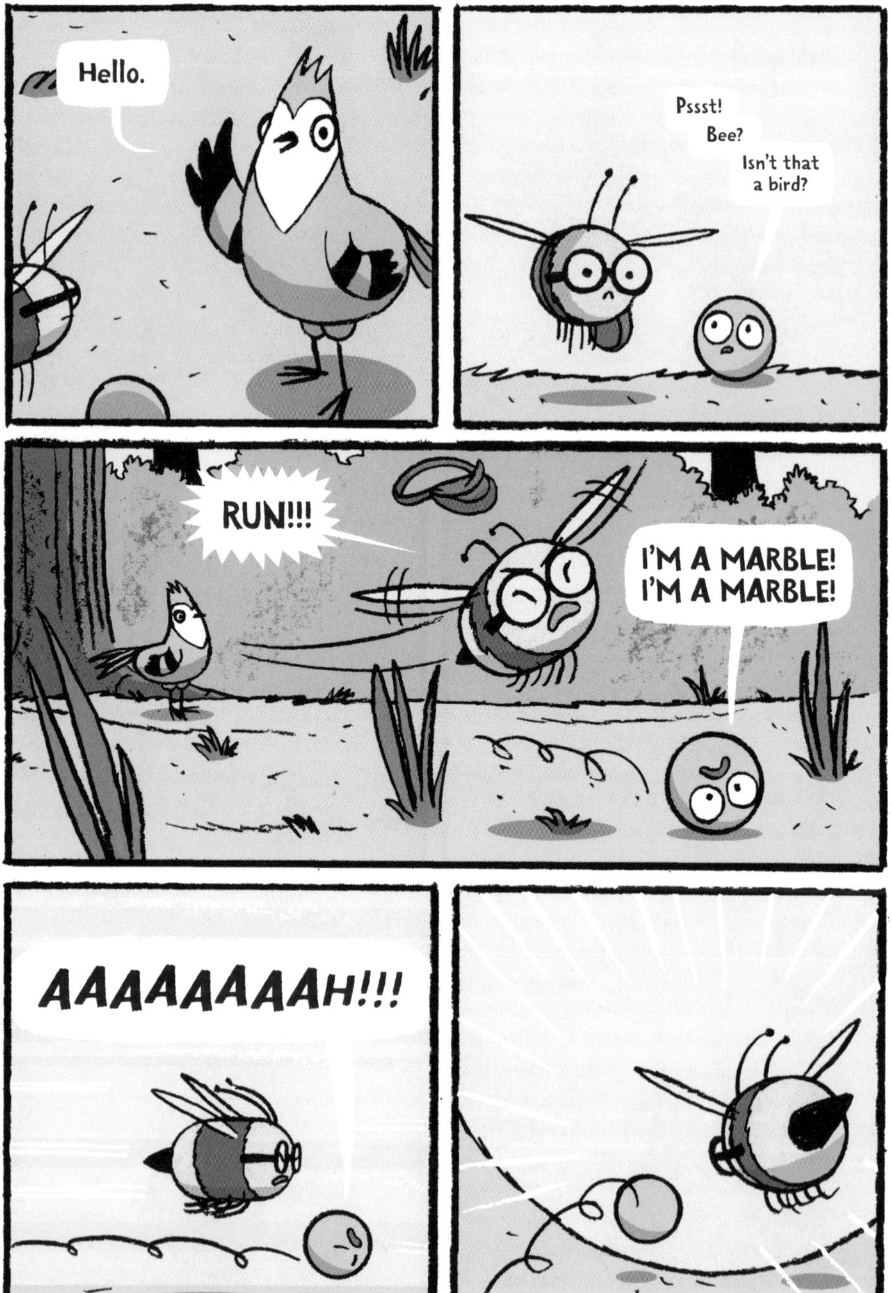
Hello.
Pssst!
Bee?
Isn't that a bird?
RUN!!!
I'M A MARBLE! I'M A MARBLE!
AAAAAAAAH!!!

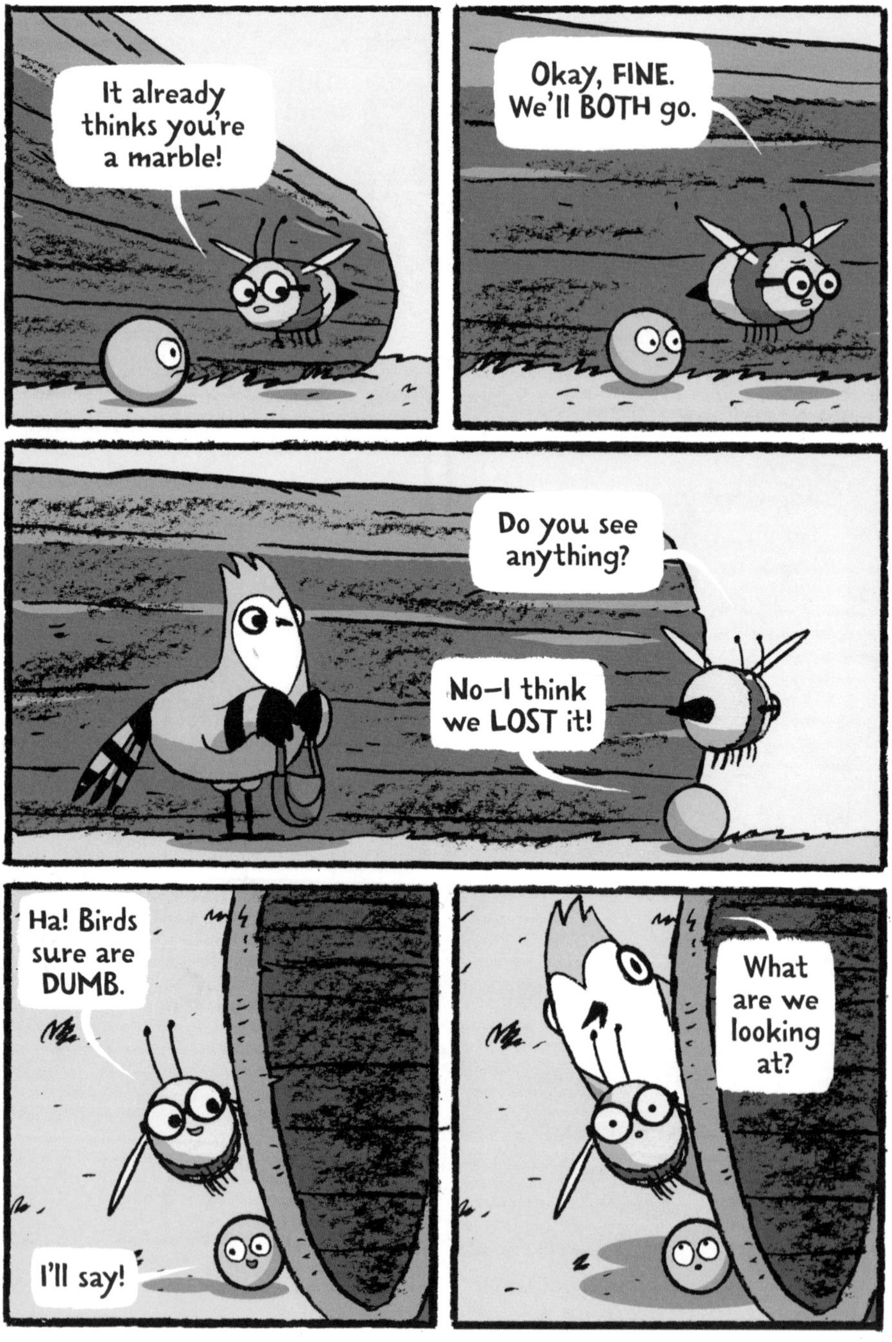
It already thinks you're a marble!
Okay, FINE. We'll BOTH go.
Do you see anything?
No—I think we LOST it!
Ha! Birds sure are DUMB.
I'll say!
What are we looking at?

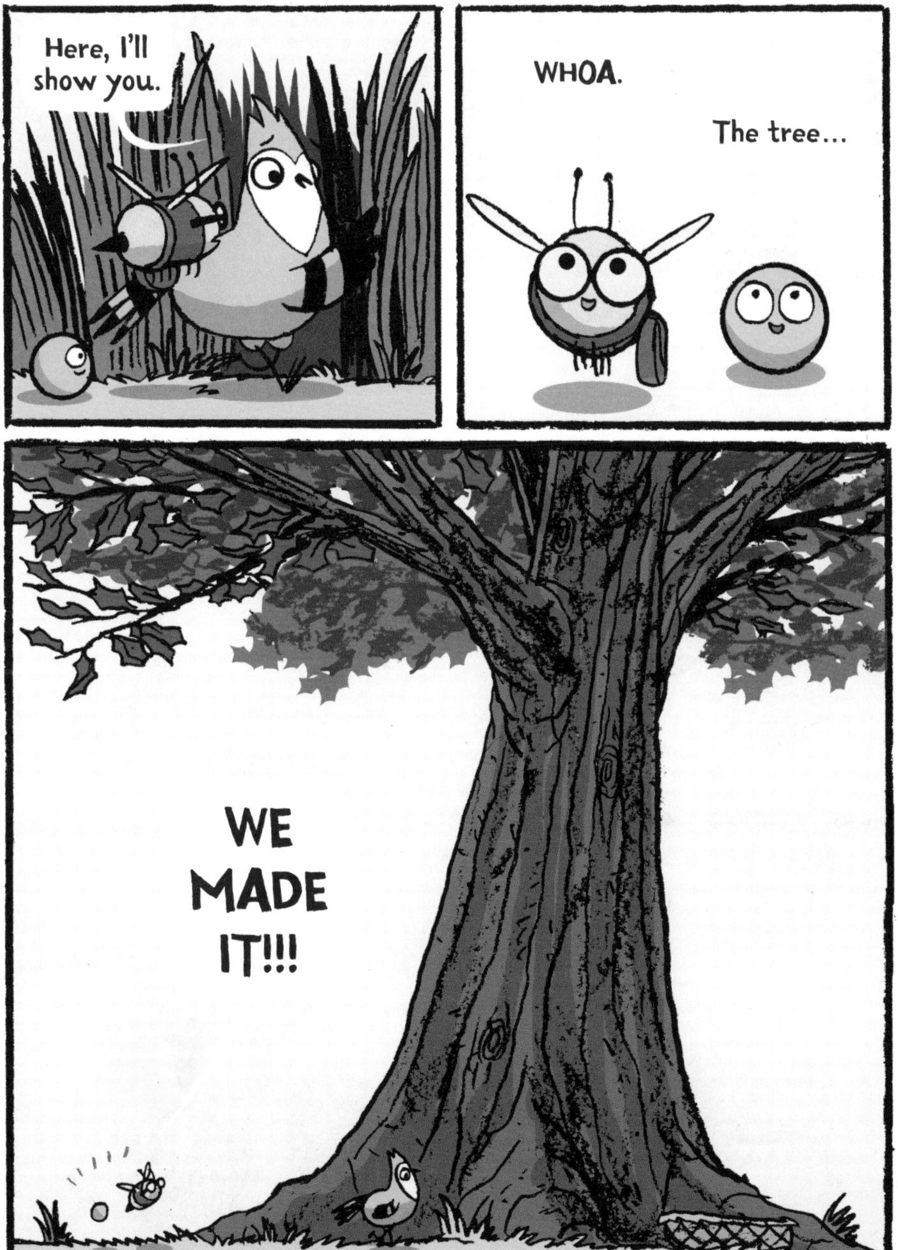
Here, I'll show you.
WHOA.
The tree...
WE MADE IT!!!

31

33

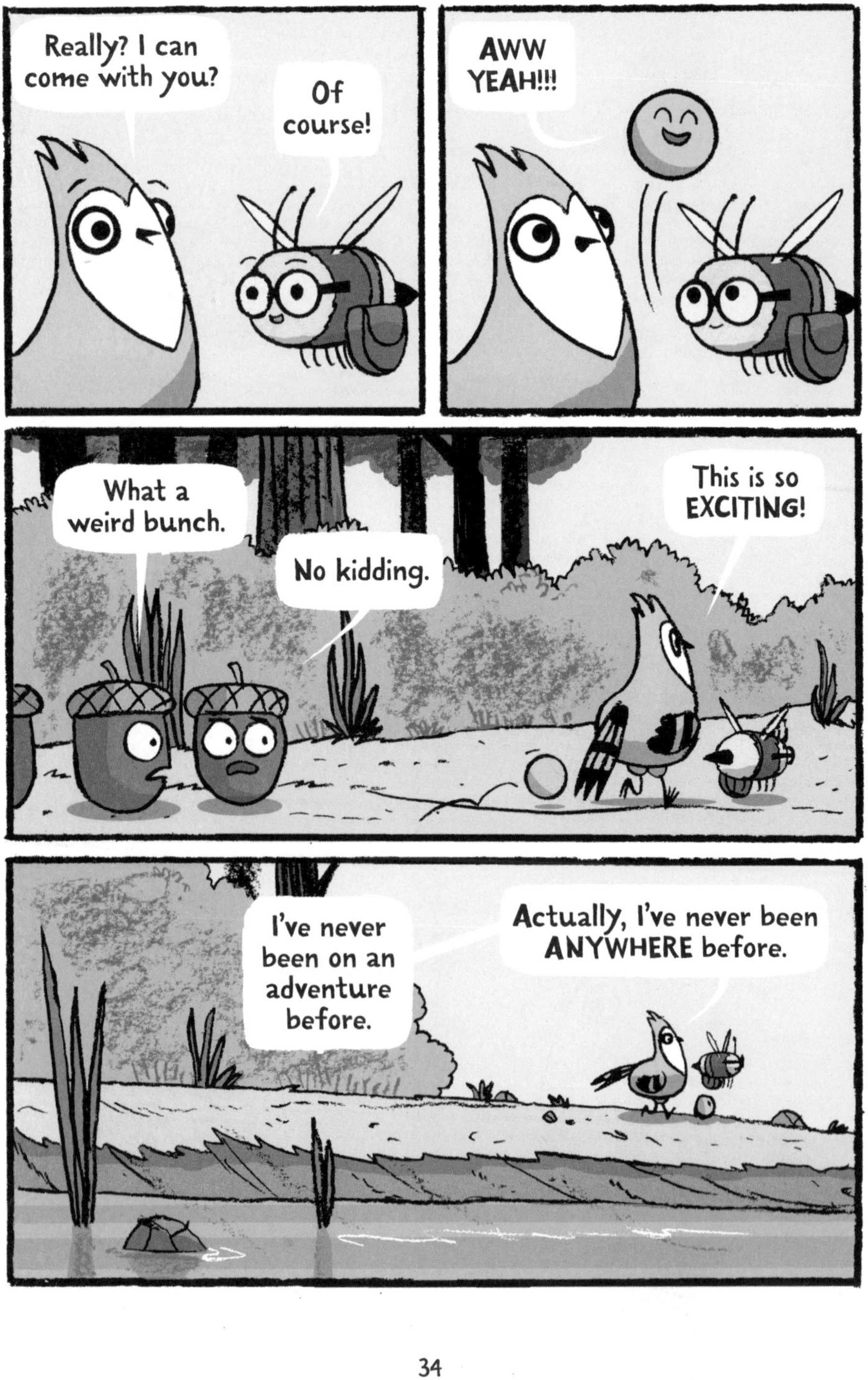
Really? I can come with you?
Of course!
AWW YEAH!!!
What a weird bunch.
No kidding.
This is so EXCITING!
I've never been on an adventure before.
Actually, I've never been ANYWHERE before.

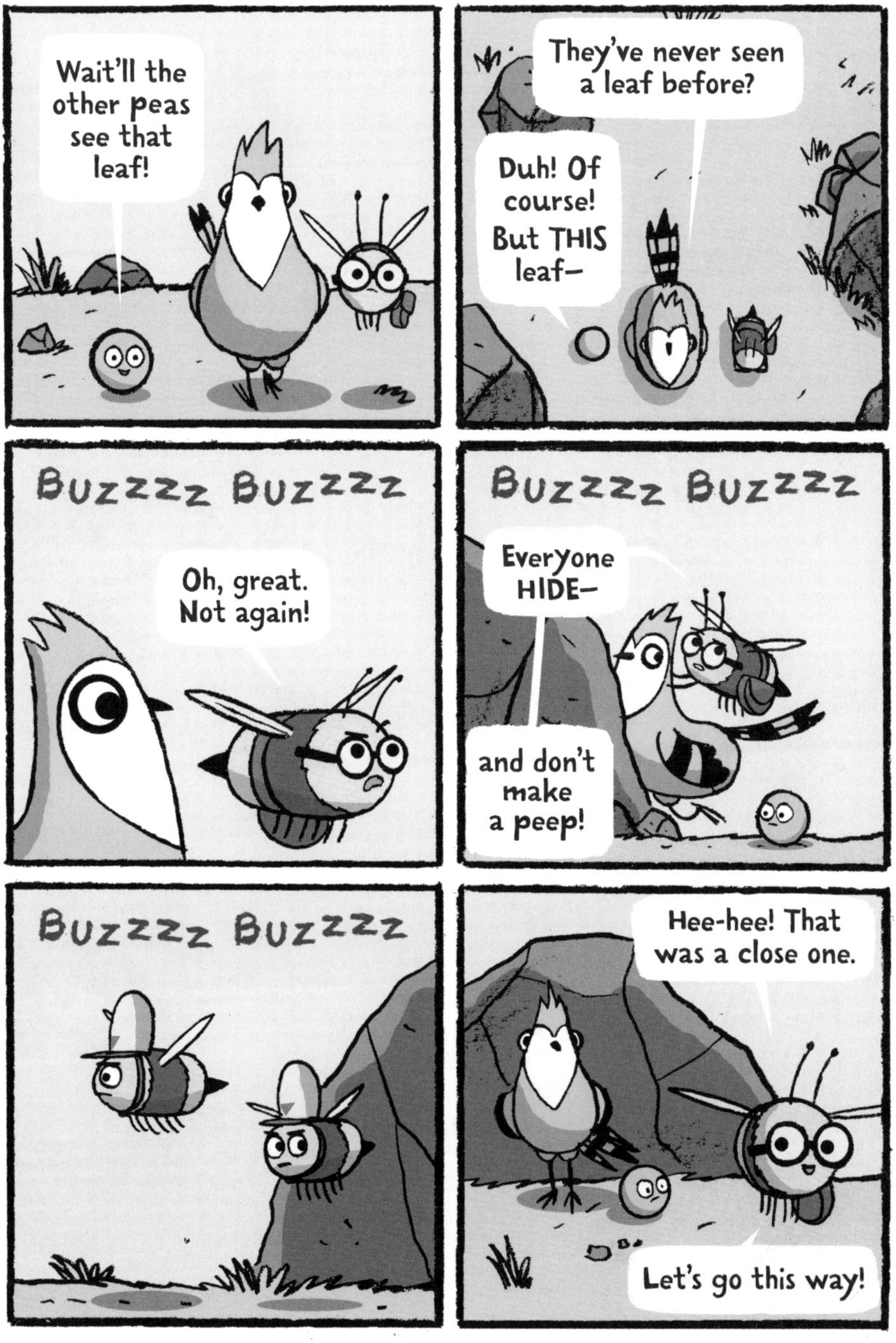
Wait'll the other peas see that leaf!
They've never seen a leaf before?
Duh! Of course! But THIS leaf—
BUZZZZ BUZZZZ
Oh, great. Not again!
BUZZZZ BUZZZZ
Everyone HIDE—
and don't make a peep!
BUZZZZ BUZZZZ
Hee-hee! That was a close one.
Let's go this way!

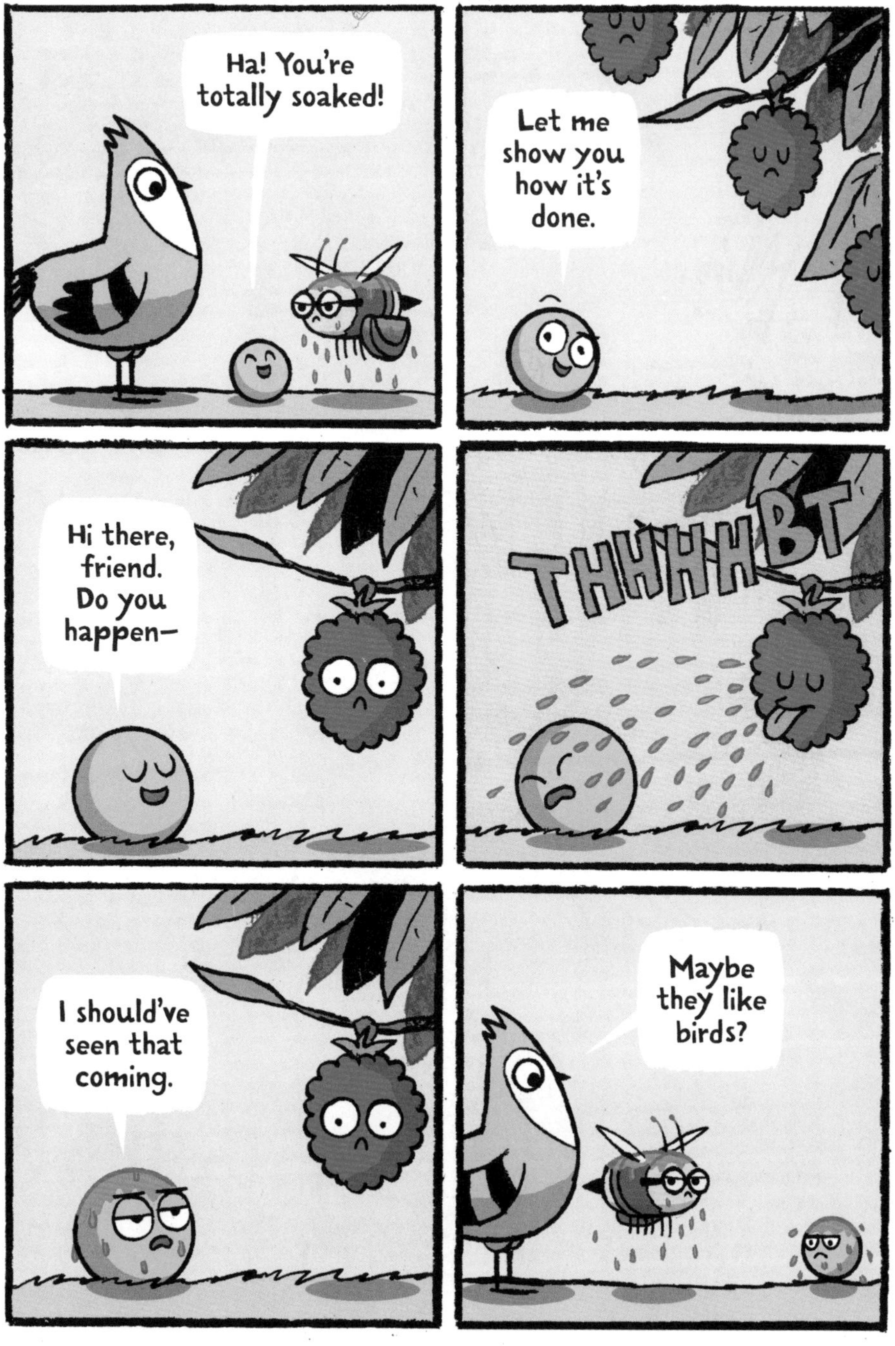
Ha! You're totally soaked!
Let me show you how it's done.
Hi there, friend. Do you happen—
THHHHBT
I should've seen that coming.
Maybe they like birds?

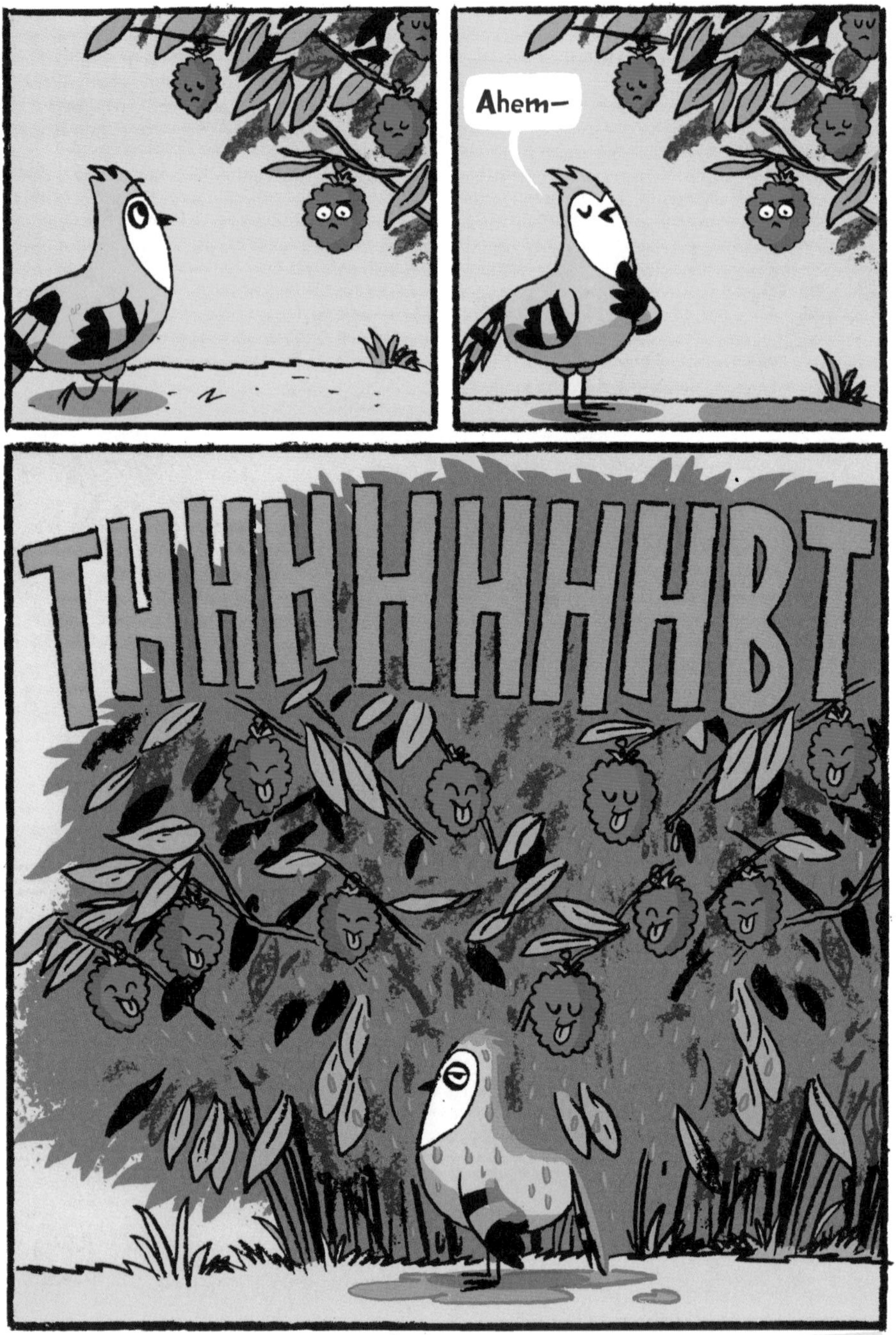
Ahem–
THHHHHHHBT

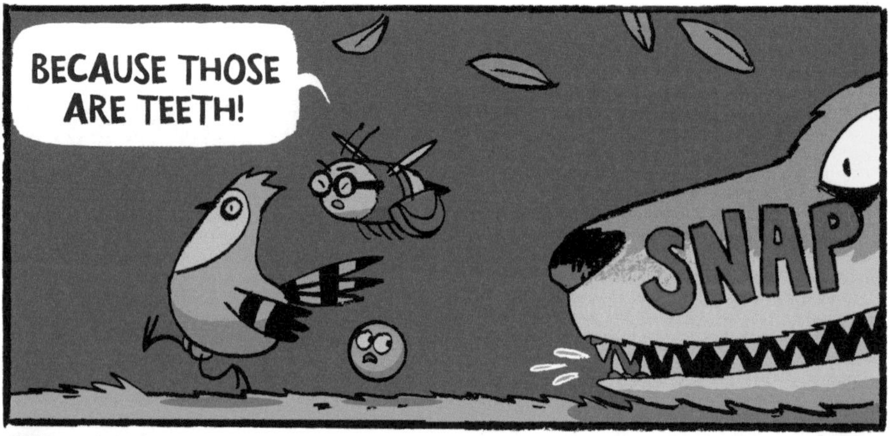
BECAUSE THOSE ARE TEETH!
SNAP

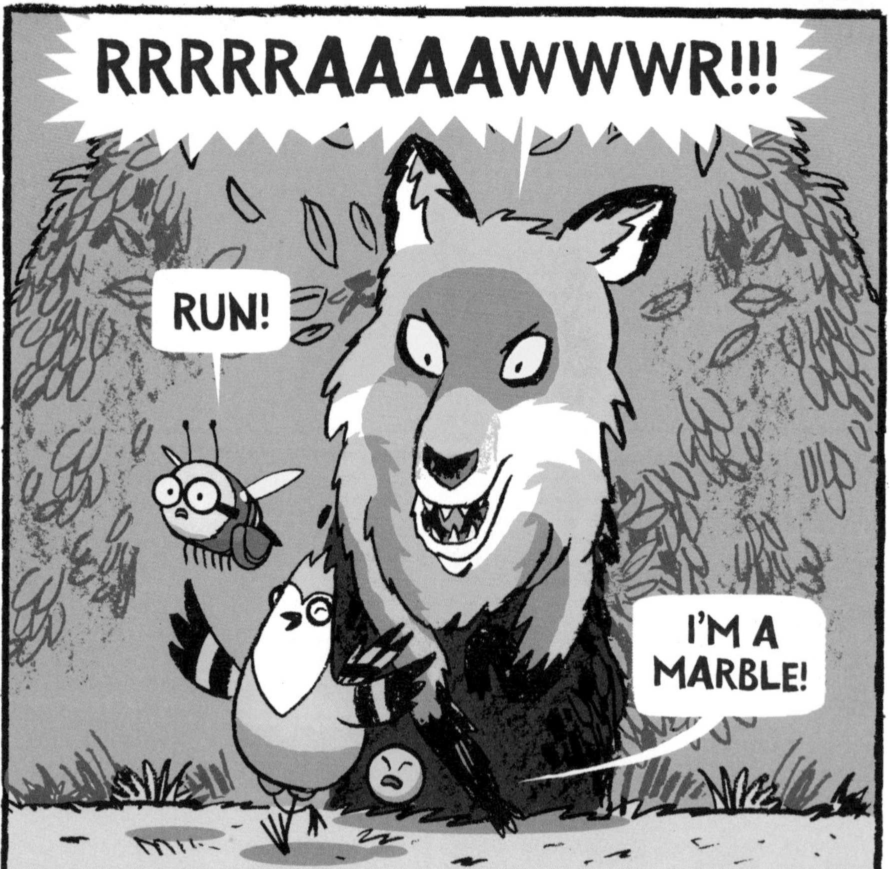
RRRRRAAAAWWWR!!!
RUN!
I'M A MARBLE!

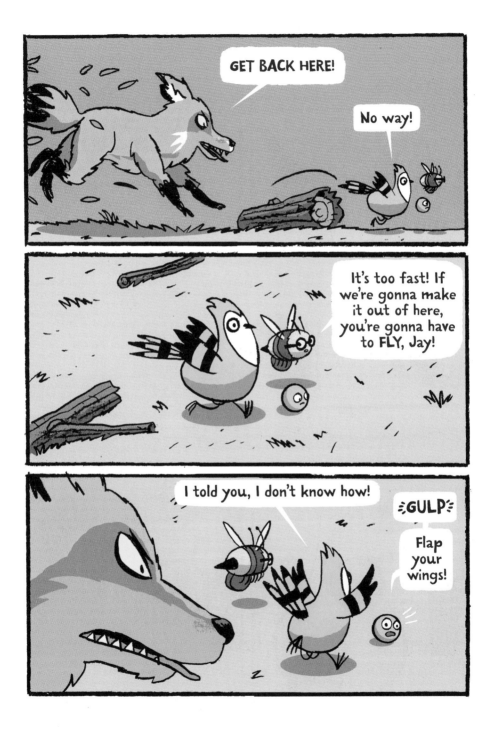

43

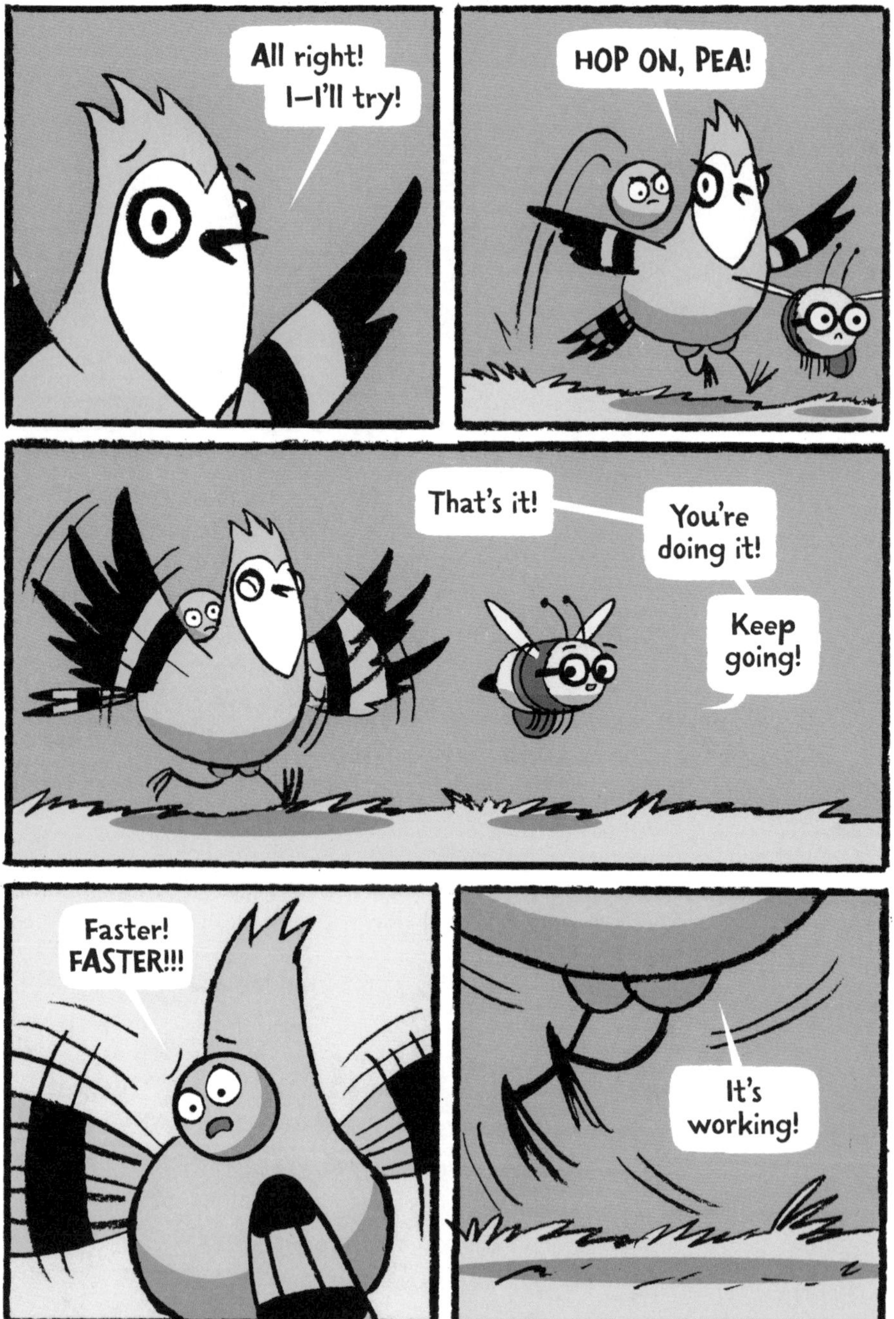
All right! I–I'll try!
HOP ON, PEA!
That's it!
You're doing it!
Keep going!
Faster! FASTER!!!
It's working!

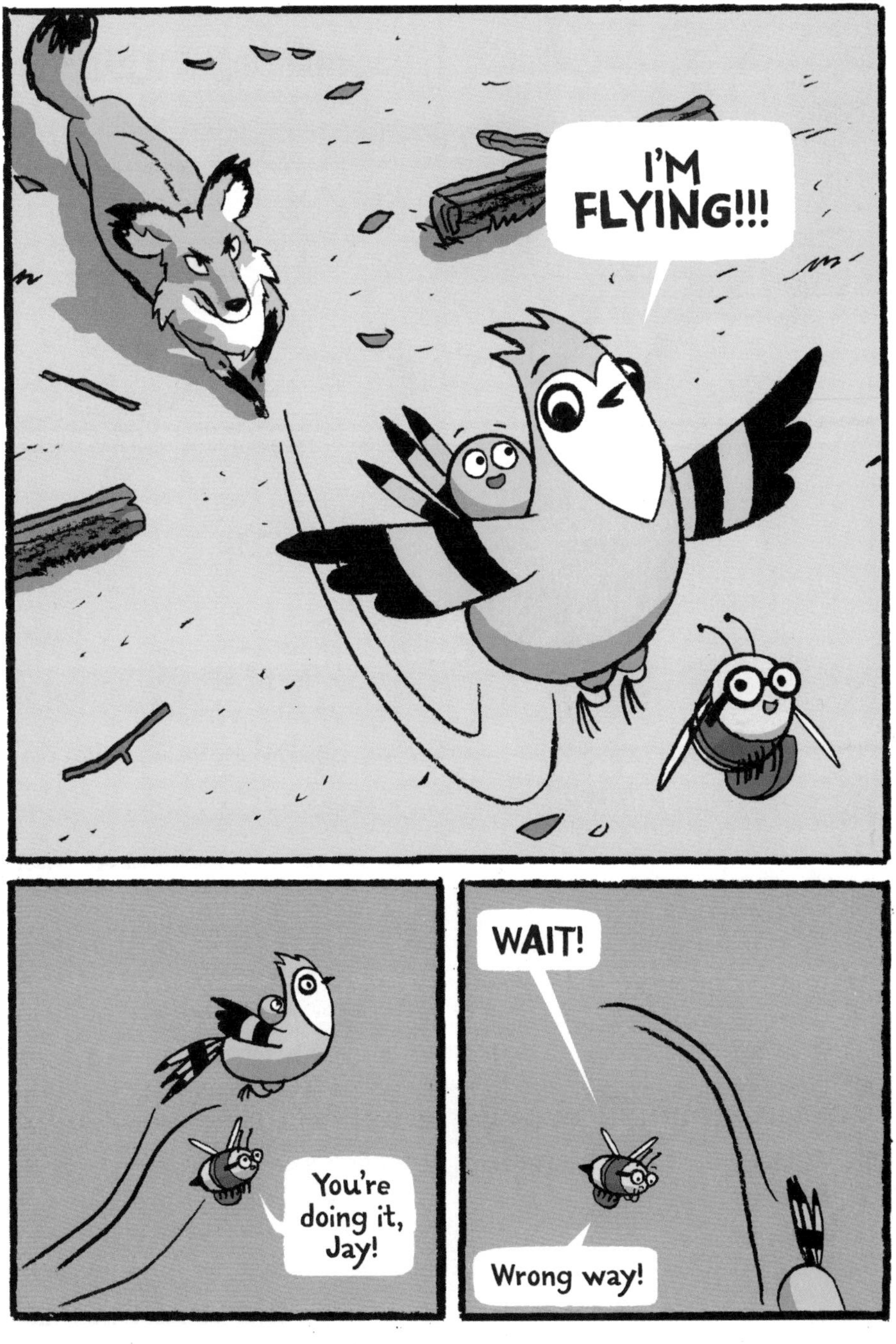
I'M FLYING!!!
You're doing it, Jay!
WAIT!
Wrong way!

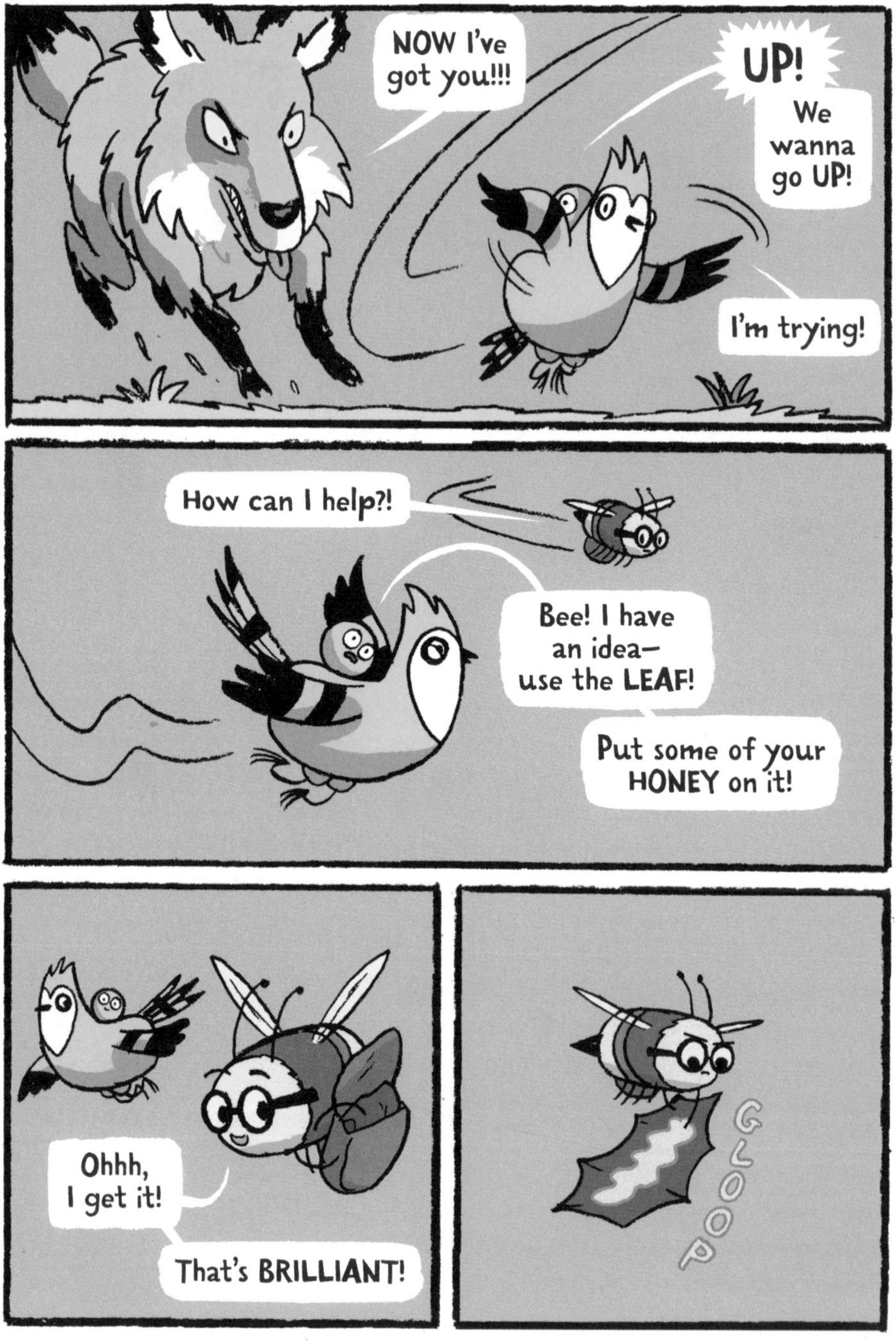
NOW I've got you!!!
UP!
We wanna go UP!
I'm trying!
How can I help?!
Bee! I have an idea— use the LEAF!
Put some of your HONEY on it!
Ohhh, I get it!
That's BRILLIANT!
GLOOOP

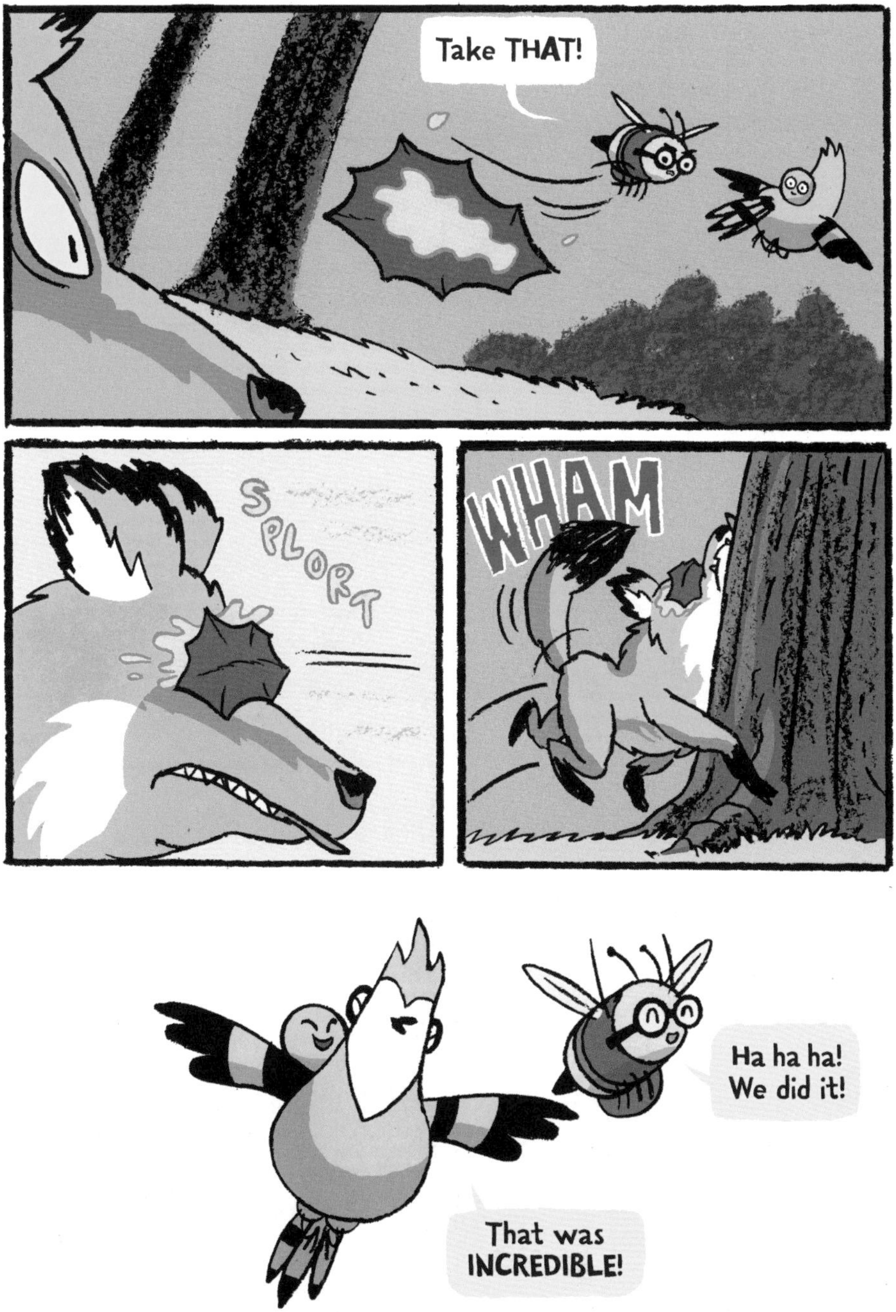
Take THAT!
SPLORT
WHAM
Ha ha ha!
We did it!
That was
INCREDIBLE!

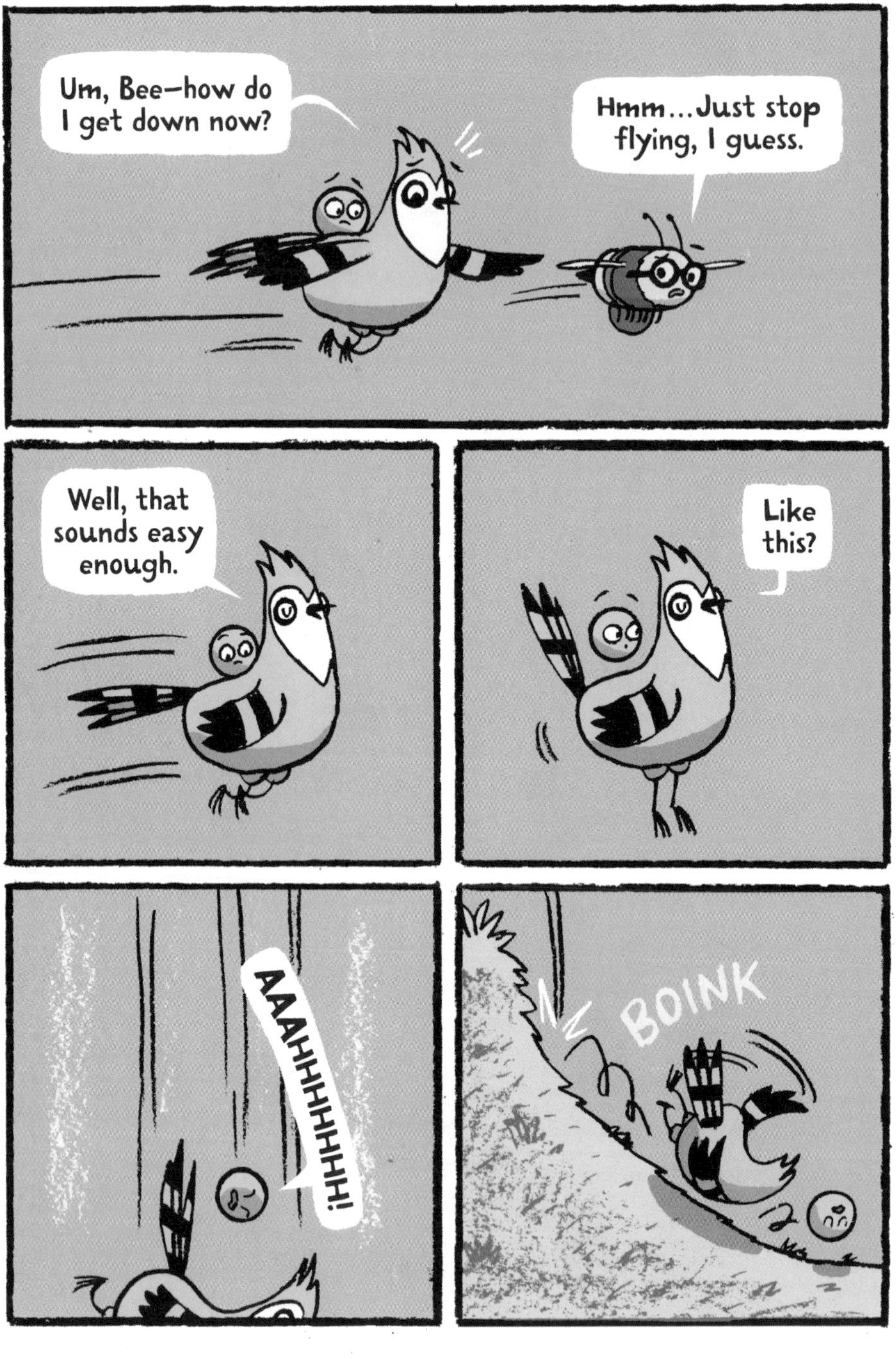
Um, Bee—how do I get down now?
Hmm...Just stop flying, I guess.
Well, that sounds easy enough.
Like this?
AAAHHHHHHH!
BOINK

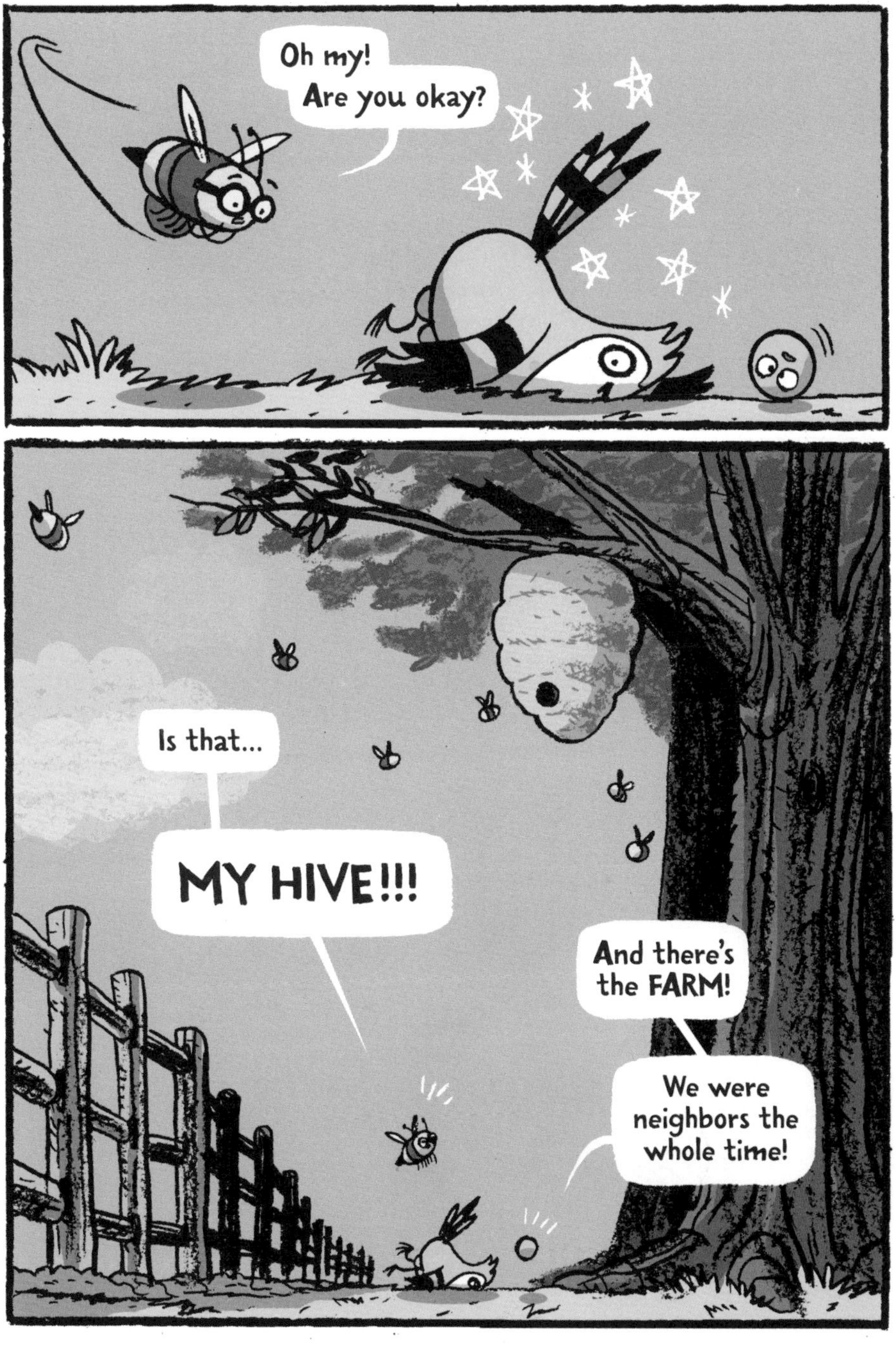
Oh my!
Are you okay?
Is that...
MY HIVE!!!
And there's the FARM!
We were neighbors the whole time!

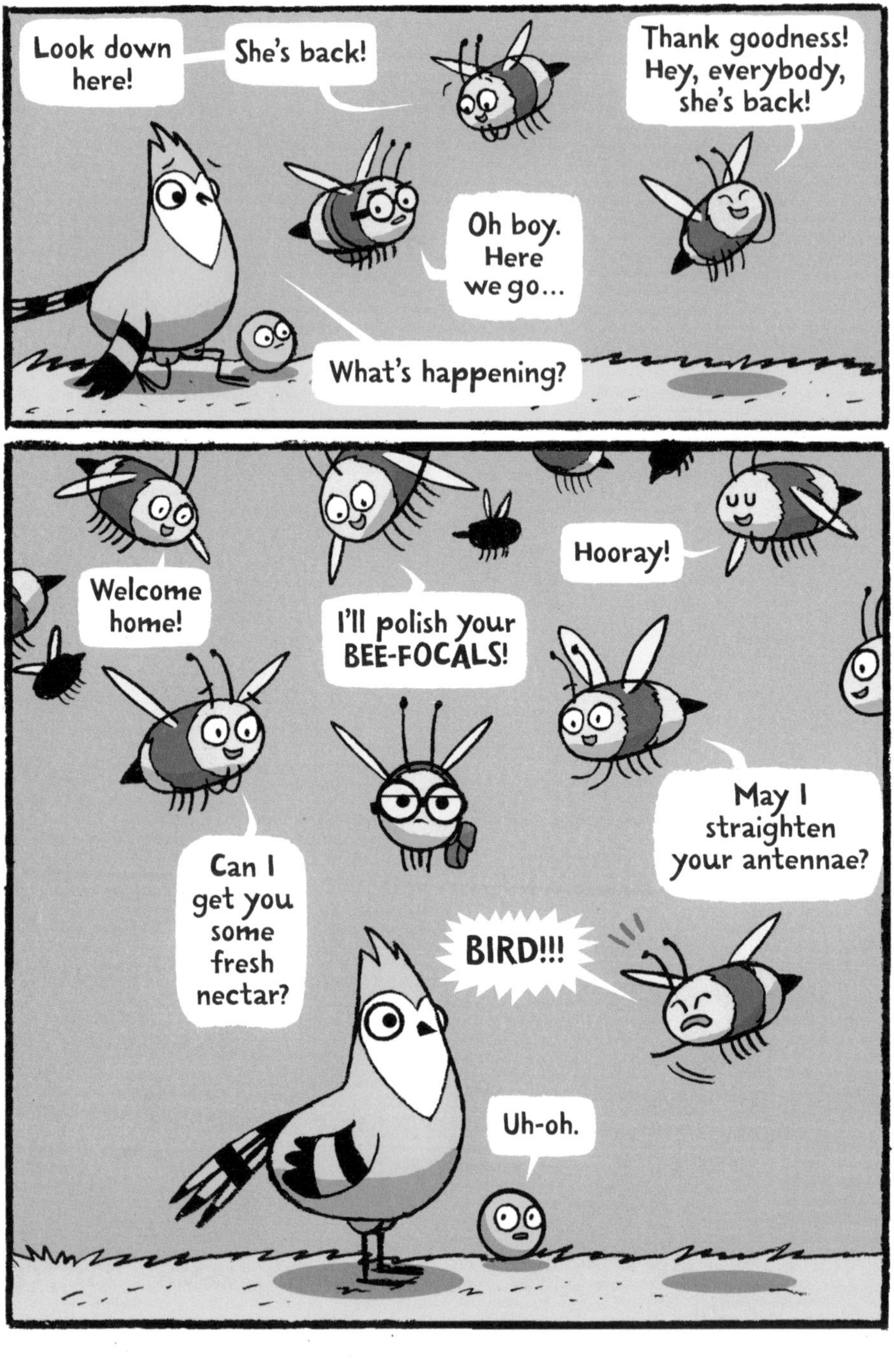
Look down here!
She's back!
Thank goodness! Hey, everybody, she's back!
Oh boy. Here we go...
What's happening?
Welcome home!
I'll polish your BEE-FOCALS!
Hooray!
May I straighten your antennae?
Can I get you some fresh nectar?
BIRD!!!
Uh-oh.

53

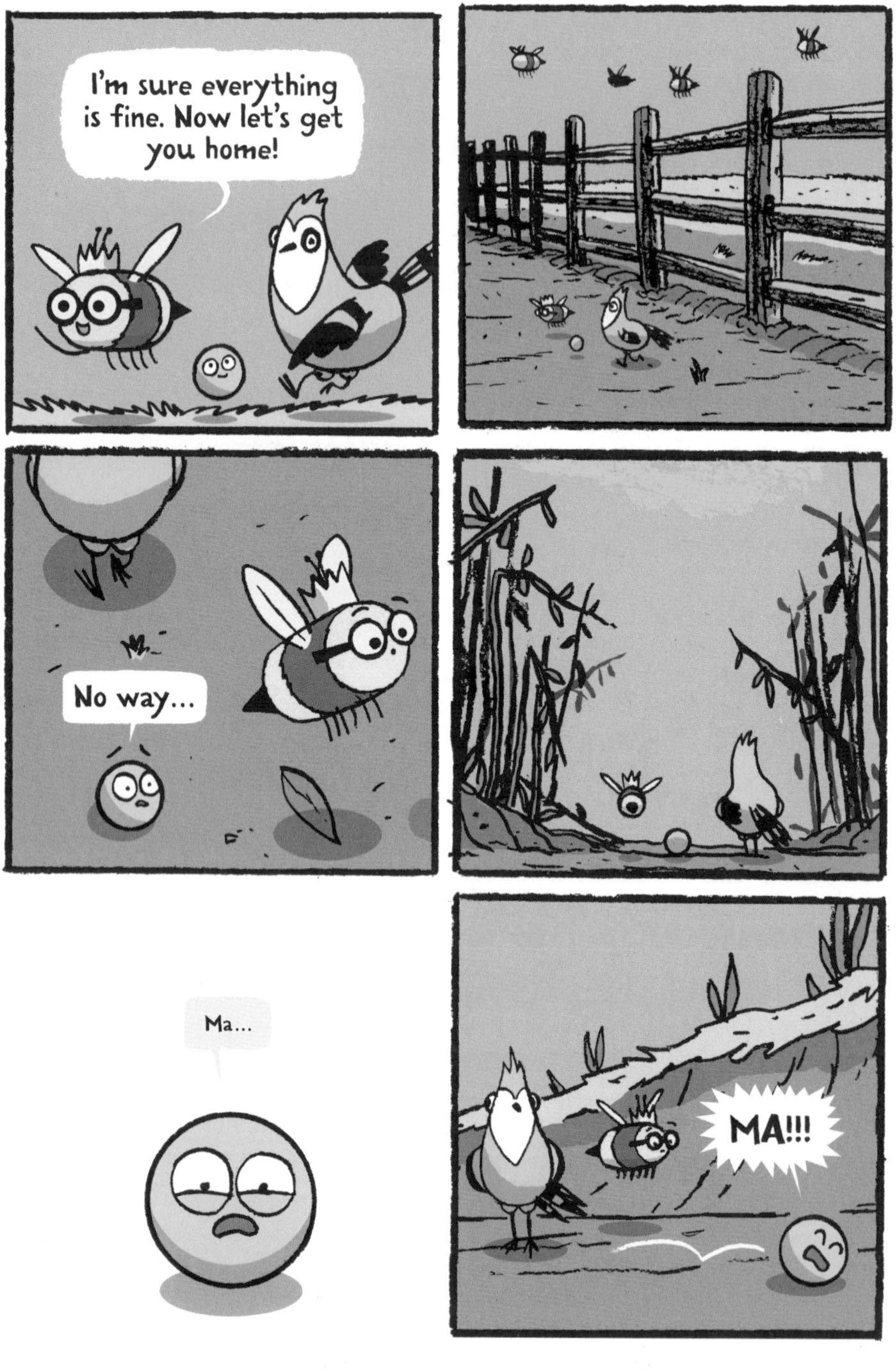
I'm sure everything is fine. Now let's get you home!
No way...
Ma...
MA!!!

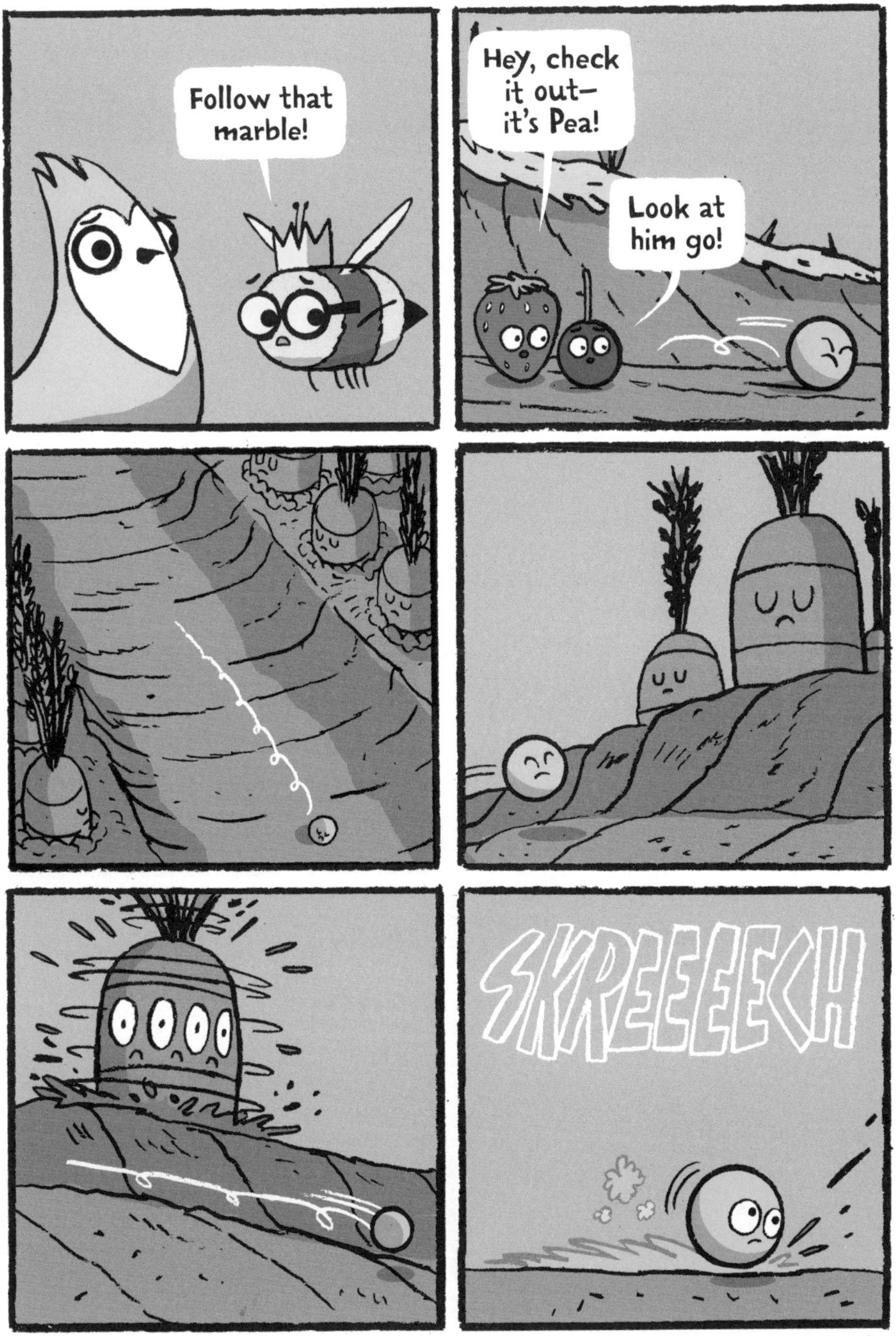
Follow that marble!
Hey, check it out— it's Pea!
Look at him go!
SKREEEEECH

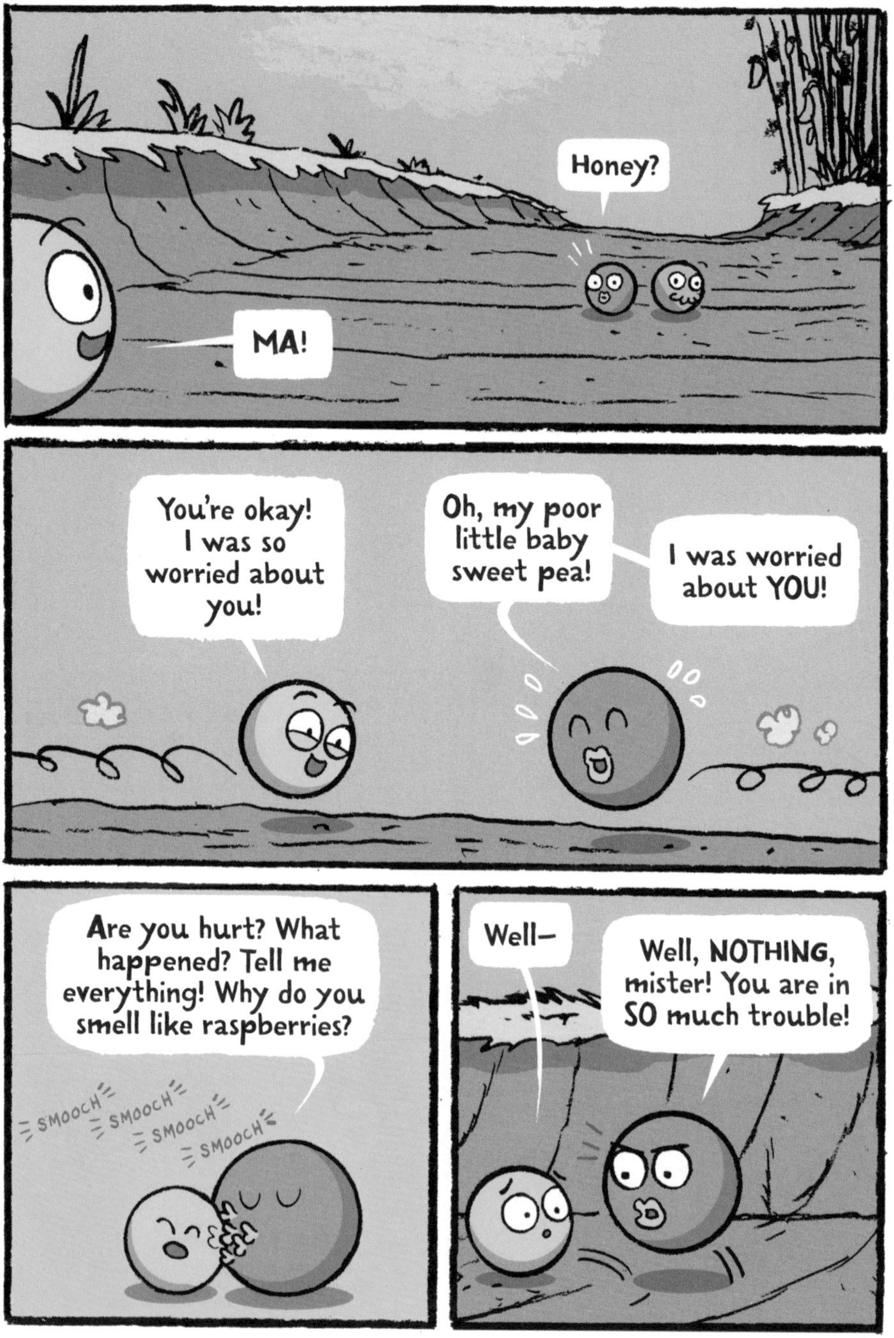
Honey?
MA!
You're okay! I was so worried about you!
Oh, my poor little baby sweet pea!
I was worried about YOU!
Are you hurt? What happened? Tell me everything! Why do you smell like raspberries?
SMOOCH
SMOOCH
SMOOCH
SMOOCH
Well—
Well, NOTHING, mister! You are in SO much trouble!

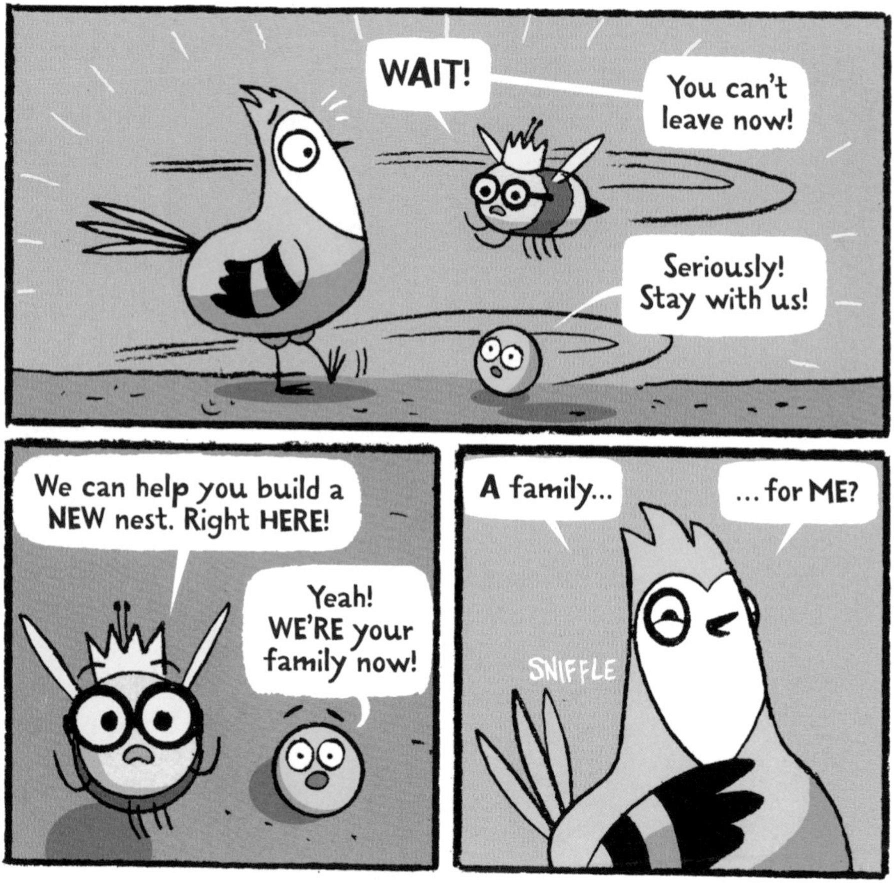
WAIT!
You can't leave now!
Seriously! Stay with us!
We can help you build a NEW nest. Right HERE!
Yeah! WE'RE your family now!
A family...
... for ME?
SNIFFLE

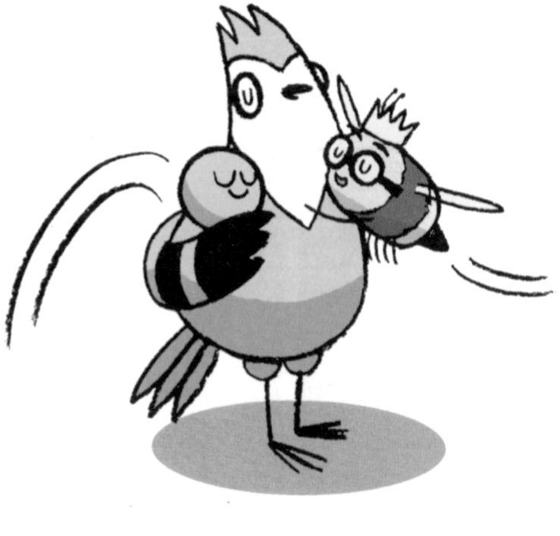

Thank you to Bret Parks, Juliet Parks, Elise Parks,
Robin Parks, and Ssalefish Comics, without whom
this book would not have been possible.

HarperAlley is an imprint of HarperCollins Publishers.

Pea, Bee, & Jay #1: Stuck Together
Copyright © 2020 by Brian Smith
All rights reserved. Printed in Slovenia.

Library of Congress Control Number: 2019953352
ISBN 978-0-06-298117-2 — ISBN 978-0-06-298116-5 (pbk.)

The artist used pencils, paper, a computer, and bee poop (lots and lots
of bee poop) to create the digital illustrations for this book.
Typography by Erica De Chavez and Andrew Arnold
20 21 22 23 24   GPS   10 9 8 7 6 5 4 3 2 1
❖
First Edition